MW01254033

BODY COUNT

BODY COUNT

A Killer Collection

Darrell James

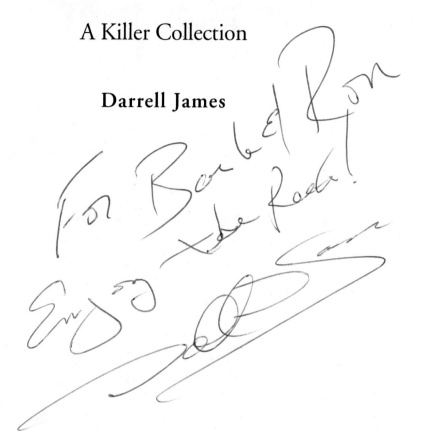

For Barb & Ed Ryan
Enjoy the Ride!

iUniverse, Inc.

New York Lincoln Shanghai

BODY COUNT
A Killer Collection

Copyright © 2006 by Darrell James

All rights reserved. No part of this book may be used or reproduced by any means, graphic, electronic, or mechanical, including photocopying, recording, taping or by any information storage retrieval system without the written permission of the publisher except in the case of brief quotations embodied in critical articles and reviews.

iUniverse books may be ordered through booksellers or by contacting:

iUniverse
2021 Pine Lake Road, Suite 100
Lincoln, NE 68512
www.iuniverse.com
1-800-Authors (1-800-288-4677)

ISBN-13: 978-0-595-37783-1 (pbk)
ISBN-13: 978-0-595-82157-0 (ebk)
ISBN-10: 0-595-37783-1 (pbk)
ISBN-10: 0-595-82157-X (ebk)

Printed in the United States of America

This book is dedicated to Tom Ogle for trusting in me enough to marry his daughter those many years ago. And to his wife Lori. Also, special thanks to GinELF for her talent and generous spirit. You can find her at: Gin@ArtbyGinELF.com

Contents

▼

INTRODUCTION

Murder—it's been played out millions of times in life, and in storytelling, through the media of books, television, and movies. Sometimes violent, sometimes gory, sometimes no more than a peaceful slide into darkness, our fascination for the topic never wanes.

What intrigues me most is not the act of murder, but the logic—the rationale—that leads to it. Specifically, at what point during the course of human conflict does the mind decide—actually decide—that murder is a rational option. At what moment does homicide reasonably become the solution of choice?

In the fifteen stories framed between these covers, I have attempted to capture that moment, along with a roadmap of the influences that shape the reasoning for this ultimate decision.

The human mind can run to dark places: misguided passion, irreconcilable pride, undeniable anger, or just plain greed. Take the stories in order or pull from the titles that intrigue you. Step inside the minds of everyday people—a priest; a senior citizen; a recovering alcoholic; an ex-con photographer—then perhaps you'll see, that in the end, all murders are "justifiable homicide"…at least, in the minds of the killers.

LYDIA

She was worth killing for.

The idea occurred to me as I lay on damp sheets amid the smell of perfume and sweat, and listened to her retreating footfalls down the stairs. Hearing the door to her quarters latch softly behind her, I thought it once more... *Worth killing my wife, Marla, for; worth any risk a man might take.*

She was our housekeeper, Lydia. Dark Lydia. Exotic Lydia. Ravenous Lydia. We had been engaged in our carnal couplings for more than a month now. Lydia would come to me like a feverish apparition, urgent and hungry. And, as Marla slept only a room away, she would thrust her nightly madness upon me until Marla's first stirrings could be heard. Then she would slip quietly down the stairs to her room. It would be hours—long painful hours—before she would return to me again.

Lydia had been Marla's idea. Hire a housekeeper to unburden her from the mundane trappings of laundry and dirty dishes. It was all part of Marla's master plan to live the perfect life. Totally consistent, she pointed out, with moving into a *virtual community* where leisure is the name of the game. It would allow more time to live our lives plugged-in, she'd said.

"Plugged-in!" It was what we called being logged into the psychodrome.

Psychodromes were the latest fad for the obscenely rich and famous. They were small, but indulgently expensive homes. Fully computerized, their living quarters offered the latest advancements in virtual reality. Integrated to each member of the household through a small microchip implanted beneath the hairline, the psychodrome's computer could actually read one's imagination, process the mental concepts, and play them back at large, within the drome, in a Surroundview/Surroundsound system of holographic imagery. Sophisticated feedback systems provided the sensations of smell, touch, and taste. *So real*, the brochures read, *you won't be able to tell where imagination ends and life begins.* It was a fantasy machine, pure and simple, nicely equipped. We had purchased our Drome shortly after Marla's inheritance.

The move to the Psychodrome had promised a perfectly fantastic lifestyle; promised the added advantage of bringing couples closer together inside their perfectly imagined world. But it had not, as it turned out, brought Marla and me closer. Despite the warning on the front door that read: *Caution, Over Indulgence in Psycho-Fantasy May Become Addictive*, Marla had insisted on plugging-in the moment she reached the front door. "Why have it," she reasoned, "if you don't use it?" I, on the other hand, had found the experience tiring, having always to think up some new fantasy to live-out each evening.

Yes, it had been interesting at first. But the demands it placed on the imagination, my God. I tried going along with it for a while, mostly letting Marla plug-in and take the lead. She always claimed to have more imagination than me. At these times I would simply sit back and let her do the mental driving, making myself something of a passenger on Marla's train of thought. But even that, too, grew tiresome.

Night-after-night we lived through one lurid fantasy or another. I longed for a normal interaction, and when it didn't come, at last, I exploded.

The argument drove us apart and I began sleeping in one of the guest bedrooms. Marla continued her nightly forays into fantasy. She tried to make amends, telling me I should just give it another chance, try concentrating for a change. But I just couldn't bring myself to reverse field. And it was for sure she wasn't going to give up that damned machine. She was hooked good, addicted to the pleasures of the drome. We were at an impasse. And her suggestion of hiring a housekeeper so she would have more time for it just further aggravated our relationship. I began to think about leaving, alone…then Lydia arrived.

God, she was beautiful! If I could have imagined such a creature, the image would have fallen short: dark, exotic, mysterious. A jungle cat with a windblown mane of hair and black pearl-drop eyes that cut to the soul. She came to me almost at once, leaving me physically depleted and mystified by her presence. Night-after-night she returned. I began to forget about Marla and her fantasy machine. I had Lydia: beautiful Lydia, responsive Lydia, *real* Lydia. But she was only for the night and I wanted more. I thought of her every waking minute, obsessed over her. She was a drug that I could not put down.

When I could no longer endure the torment, I confessed to Marla and sought dissolution of the marriage. She laughed. "Have your fun, dear," she told me, "but you can't go anywhere with Lydia, silly."

Now the idea of killing Marla loomed large in front of me. Lydia and I living together both night and day.

I planned it throughout the morning: wait until nightfall, I decided, use the cover of darkness to dispose of her body. Perhaps bury her in the back yard. Why not? The possibilities were titillating. *Real* was the word that came to mind. Quite better than plugging-in and dreaming such a thing.

I waited for darkness to settle in, then retrieving my ball peen hammer from my toolbox I made my way to Marla's room. I found her lying face-up on her bed, eyes closed. But was she sleeping? I didn't think so. She could be plugged-in, dreaming some intoxicating fantasy. But the house appeared normal, no holographic images dancing before me. No unusual sensations.

I looked at Marla's face there on the bed. Not a bad face really: smooth and pleasant. Perhaps a bit pasty, but it had a sweet and kind turn to it. She had always been good to me—I'd give her that. But she was not Lydia: dark, intoxicating Lydia.

I turned my hammer with the ball peen facing forward. Then brought it over and down in a wide swift arc. It struck Marla square in the forehead with a dull pumpkin-thump sound. Her eyes popped open momentarily, then slowly sank closed. A deep dent was rendered in her skull above the ridge of her brow. There was a starburst pattern of blood radiating from its center. A small pool of blood filled the hole and ran toward her eyelids. It was done.

There was a moment of remorse and regret, but my thoughts turned swiftly to Lydia. I swelled with the idea of seeing her now, ached with the prospect of telling her of my deed and informing her that we now had all eternity to spend together. No more sneaking-in during the dark of night, no more slipping-off in the gray of dawn. Overcome with elation I rushed from Marla's bedroom to join Lydia.

The first troubling concerns came to me as I reached the end of the hallway where the staircase would begin. The stairs were no longer there, but rather a doorway that led to the family room. I raced through the room, knocking over the end table and lamp in my haste. I re-exited into the dining area, passed through and into the kitchen and out. The route brought me full circle, back to the end of the hallway where I'd begun. The room where I'd been sleeping and rendezvousing nightly with Lydia lay just ahead down the hallway. And farther down, at the end was the master bedroom, Marla's.

A single nagging thought tapped at my subconscious. It continued tapping then begun banging until, at last, I was forced to acknowledge it. A sudden realization set-in and with it a wave of sickness and nausea that threatened to drag me to the floor...

We had purchased the single-story Drome.

There were no stairs. And, if there were no stairs, there was no maid's quarters at the landing.

I checked my hand for the hammer. It was still in my grip, blood dripped from the head. Down the hallway, past the open door to the master bedroom, I could see Marla's body stretched in repose. Blood had pooled in her eye sockets and had run off to stain the sheets. I heard Marla's voice inside my head: "Have your fun, dear. But you can't go anywhere with Lydia, silly."

And now I understood.

Lydia was Marla's fantasy. Created, likely, to satisfy me. Her attempt to keep me happy. Her attempt to keep me from going away.

I now spend my days, as well as my nights, plugged-in to our home—the Psychodrome. Marla's body still lies on the bed, growing riper by the day. Perhaps I'll find something to do with her tomorrow.

In the meantime, I try with all my might to draw Lydia back in fantasy. Dark Lydia...soft Lydia...wild Lydia...passionate Lydia...voluptuous Lydia...

But with each passing day my hope dwindles.

There's a truth involved here, I'm coming to realize...Marla always did have more imagination than me.

Lydia first appeared in the 2004 Autumn Issue of Futures Mysterious Anthology Magazine.

FREMONT & LOUGIE

Getting the man into the trunk of the car was harder than they'd figured. He didn't want to go.

"Man, push his leg down!" Fremont said. "Push it down!"

"It won't go! He keeps stiffenin' up!" Lougie told him.

The man was dressed in his bathrobe, a pair of wingtip shoes they'd let him slip on. He was gagged and his hands were tied behind his back. Inside his foot-hills home, at gunpoint, he had cooperated fully. Now, in the driveway, in the dark, at the prospect of being stuffed into the trunk of their car, he was making a fuss. There were sandwich wrappers, beer bottles, smelly oil rags in there. A couple of empty anti-freeze containers. No place for a City Councilman.

"Man, you're just making it hard on yourself," Fremont told the man. "Don't make me get my gun out and bust you right here."

They held him like a sack of feed, hairy legs showing outside his boxers. Fremont had him under the arms, while Lougie wrestled with the feet. Christ, he was heavy. And bucking the way he was.

"Hey, damn!" Lougie cried, losing his grip, the man's one leg coming free to kick out. It caught Lougie hard in the teeth. Lougie howled, grappling to bring the free leg back under control.

"You want to keep it down!" Fremont scolded. "You gonna wake the neighbors."

"But, he kicked me," Lougie whined.

"One thing you gotta do—shit!—is hang on to the man's legs. Now, come on. On three. One…two…three!"

They got their momentum up and this time hefted the man up and into the trunk. Fremont quickly rolled the man facedown and sat on his shoulders, while Lougie bent the knees and stuffed the rest inside. They jammed the lid shut, hearing the man cursing behind his gag.

"Man's bigger than he looks on TV," Fremont said, huffing to catch his breath. "I could use a drink."

"I think he loosened my tooth," Lougie said, testing a molar with his index finger. "I think my lip's busted, maybe."

"Man, just be happy porch lights didn't start comin' on, or more than that would get busted. Come on, let's get this over with."

The man in the bathrobe they'd seen on television the week before: Councilman Abe Hornackey speaking out about rampant, unchecked land development and threatening to put a stop to it. It was followed by a clip that showed a developer from New Jersey, named Jimmy Nuccio, who was ranting publicly and declaring war against the Councilman for his attitudes. It gave Fremont an idea.

"Man's Italian," he told Lougie, the two of them smoking jays at Fremont's apartment. "Know what they call him? They call him, Jimmy Nuts."

"Yeah, so?" Lougie said.

"Man's connected," Fremont said. "Which means he's probably into bribes, payoffs, shit like that to get his cheap-ass apartments built."

Lougie shook his head, not clear where Fremont was going.

"That means, see," Fremont said, "this City Council dude is probably the only man in government that can't be bought. You know how these crusading types is. Mister Clean. And now this mobbed-up dude has just publicly made threats against him on network television."

"I don't see what that's got to do with us," Lougie said, taking short little hits on the fat boy he'd just rolled.

"Well, the way I see it, if something were to happen to this City Cat, Hornackey...say he turns up dead or permanently missing or something...the first person they gonna suspect is this Nuts guy. I mean, you know his reputation is less than cherry, just by his name. I say we kidnap the Councilman and threaten to blame it on the Nuccio guy if he don't pay us some cash."

That night, in front of the TV, their heads softened to mush on Mexican brown, Fremont had to spell it out in detail before Lougie could understand it. But, now, here they were, heading for the landfill with the Councilman in the trunk, bruising his good knees against the bumper jack.

They arrived: the landfill, to their surprise, lit up like a football field.

"I thought you said this'd be a good place," Lougie said to Fremont, looking out across barren landscape, scrapped clean by bulldozers. Chain link fencing surrounded the area. There was a maintenance trailer where the floodlights were mounted.

"There's a big pit over there they push all the garbage into. You see it in the daylight, man, you expect it to be dark at night. But it's okay. We in the middle of nowhere."

"You sure this is the best place to do it?"

"Where else you gonna leave the man, Courthouse Square? No see, they can't actually find him dead. We have to leave him someplace where he can't be found unless someone provides the proper anonymous information. Like us. That's how the threat works. Dig?"

They cut the padlock with bolt cutters from the back seat, and drove to where the pit loomed deep and dark before them.

"Knock, knock," Fremont said, opening the trunk. He had the gun out again, pointing it at the man where he was lying balled into a knot and looking up at them with wide eyes.

"You want to come out of there on your own, or you gonna make us carry you like before."

Councilman Hornackey shook his head. Hell no, he wasn't coming out.

"Now, come on," Fremont said. "Be a good boy."

When the Councilman didn't move, Fremont whacked him across the eye with the gun barrel. The man gave a muffled cry from behind the gag and cowered farther back into the littered trunk.

"Want me to smack you again?"

Hornackey shook his head.

"Then, man, come on out."

He helped the Councilman out and to his feet, then turned to Lougie. "You bring the evidence? Tell me you brought the evidence. It's no good less we can make it look like it was Jimmy Nuccio did it."

Lougie reached into his jacket pocket and came out with a second gun—this one wrapped inside a cloth bandana. He unfolded the covering and held it for Fremont to see.

"You sure this is Nuccio's gun?"

"I broke in to the man's house while he was away; took it, like you told me, from the nightstand beside the bed. You can see I was careful. Should have his fingerprints all over it."

Fremont shoved his own gun back into his waistband and took the stolen weapon, gripping it with the cloth bandana, careful not to touch the steel itself.

"All right then," Fremont said.

Lougie stole a glance over the edge, into the darkness of the pit. "You sure we have to kill him? Maybe we could just hold him hostage someplace until the man gives us the money, then let him go."

"You want to sit around spoon feedin' this yerkle for a week? Then what? Wait for the cops to show up. The man's seen our faces."

"I'm just thinking, is all."

"Well, stop it," Fremont said. "Your head makes that funny noise when you do."

Fremont turned back to find the Councilman had slipped off during the conversation. He spotted him running across the open land pack.

"Shit! Now see what you did? All that thinking."

Fremont leveled the stolen weapon and fired, nailing the Councilman with one clean shot to the middle of his back. The report echoed across the wide pit. The Councilman's knees buckled, dropping him into a fetal ball. "You see what I'm sayin'? Now we gotta carry his chunky ass again."

Instead, they dragged the Councilman to the edge of the pit, where Fremont rolled him the final distance, over and into the darkness below. The body disappeared amid the refuse, swallowed by heaped garbage bags and drifts of paper and plastic.

"Alright," Fremont said, seeming satisfied. He held the gun over the edge and let it slip from the bandana. It too disappeared, below, amid the clutter.

"We the only ones know where the body and evidence can be found," Fremont said. "Now all we got to do is see Jimmy Nuts and make sure he understands the significance of that knowledge."

The following morning they showed up at the White Horse Building—an old five story off the warehouse district—the offices of Jimmy Nuccio. Fremont had on the tan linen suit he'd bought for three dollars at Goodwill. Under it, he wore a green silk shirt. There was a stain on the cuff he kept covered by adjusting the sleeve. Lougie was in his jeans and t-shirt, his poplin jacket—same clothes as always—and dirty Converse sneakers.

In the lobby, pressing the button for the elevator and watching the numbers count down above, Fremont said, "Man, couldn't you find something better to wear."

"What's wrong with it?" Lougie asked, looking himself over.

"You look like a homeless dude. You goin' in there with your hand out? We supposed to be in charge here."

The elevator arrived and took them skyward where it deposited them into the lobby of White Horse Development. It was Saturday, the place empty. A pair of dark hallways ran off in either direction. Fish of some kind swam endless laps back and forth in a glass tank recessed into the wall behind the reception desk.

"It's quiet," Lougie said. "Maybe we should come back on Monday."

"No, man. That's the plan. I got it all worked out, see." Fremont tapped his skull with a finger. "We come on Saturday when no one else is around."

"How we know the Nuts guy is going to be here."

"There you go thinking again. I checked. He's always here on Saturdays."

Fremont ran his eyes down each of the two hallways. "I think I hear something, one of the offices down there, come on."

Fremont eased the door open to the office where window light streamed through a high, hinged transom. He poked his head inside. Lougie crowded in from behind—the two of them filling the doorway and staring now at—Christ!—walls of video monitors, banks of them, live. They filled the room from corner to corner and from floor to ceiling, different scenes on each, changing at a slow rhythmic pace. Surveillance shots: a construction site of some sort—office building maybe—workers going about their business under a watchful eye.

Jimmy Nuccio sat with his feet propped on the desk, a phone to his ear. He was a burly man with overly thick, black hair, maybe a rug. Fremont recognized him from the news clip.

Spotting the two of them bunched together in the doorway, wide-eyed with wonderment at the display before them, Nuccio said into the phone, "...hang on." He looked first at Fremont, then at Lougie, checking them out. Then his eyes came back to Fremont.

"Mop closet's down the hall," Nuccio said.

Fremont turned to Lougie. "Mop closet's down the hall. Man's a comic."

Fremont stepped fully into the room, adjusted his cuff. "Man, I come to see you."

"I'm busy. Get lost!" Nuccio said.

Jimmy Nuccio turned his attention back to the phone.

"You seen Councilman Hornackey lately?" Fremont said, floating it out there for the man, cool like, the way he'd rehearsed.

Nuccio's eyes came back around. He took Fremont in more closely now, his cool metallic gaze causing Fremont to flinch. Nuccio said into the phone, "...I'll get back to you," and hung up.

Nuccio observed the two carefully, scenes changing on the monitors behind him—workers going about their tasks. "You got something to say to me?"

Fremont crossed to take a seat in front of the desk. He crossed his legs and adjusted the pleat in his slacks. Lougie came to stand beside the chair at Fremont's side.

"What's all them?" Fremont asked, nodding toward the bank of monitors.

"Security," Nuccio said. "I watch all my job sites, beginning to end, make sure some asshole doesn't decide to walk off with a compressor, stack of lumber maybe."

"No shit, you can see them all?"

Nuccio kept his eyes on Fremont as he keyed an entry on the computer before him. The scenes changed at once. This time to a housing development: roofers tacking on asphalt shingles; carpenters banging silently away with their hammers.

"Just like that, I see it all," Nuccio said. He re-keyed the computer and the original job site came back on the screens. "And when I'm not watching, the recorders capture everything that happens."

Fremont nodded. "That's good. You're a cautious man." He was checking out a monitor where a man in a hardhat was stepping out of his vehicle. He said, "Like the dude with the pickup, load up some shit and drive off."

"Yeah, now you got something for me, Sambo, or not. I'm a busy man. What's this about Hornackey?"

"Yeah, well, as I was say…"

"Hold on," Nuccio said, raising his hand. And turning to Lougie, "You want to take a seat. Makes me nervous, you hovering."

Lougie averted his eyes, but took the extra chair and sat back. When he'd settled, Nuccio said, "Better. Go ahead."

"I was about to…" Fremont started, then had to back up, reorganize his thought. "What I mean is, I was wondering if you'd seen anything of Councilman Hornackey lately?"

Listening to himself, Fremont wanted to scream. It was supposed to come off cool, heavy-handed, instead it sounded stupid, doltish.

Nuccio looked from Fremont to Lougie, back again. Pasting a perplexed expression on his face, he said, "Am I supposed to, what?"

"No, man, shit," Fremont said. He was getting frustrated. "Councilman ain't nowhere to be seen. That's the point."

"Why didn't you just fucking say that?" Nuccio said evenly.

"The Councilman isn't coming back no more, alright!" Fremont said. "And the reason he ain't is because he's dead and was you who killed him."

Nuccio struck a pose, appearing to give it some though. "No…I don't think so. I would have remembered that. Wha

It wasn't turning out at all like Fremont had imagined—co This guy, this big-knuckled Guinea with the attention span of a . those videos—they were throwing him off his game. Lougie ...ere, hat-in-hand, the way he was, not adding anything.

Fremont came to his feet. "Looky here, man!" he said, placing his hands flat on Nuccio's desk, leaning in. "You need to shape your punk-ass and listen!"

"I don't know what that means," Nuccio said. "You want to try speaking English."

"Means you're in deep shit you don't pay attention!" Fremont was frothing now.

"Alright, alright. Sit down."

Nuccio waved Fremont back into his seat. He studied Fremont for a second then dropped his feet off the desk and came around to lean on his elbows, his attention focused on him politely. "So you popped the crusading Councilman. Tell me…what's that got to do with me?"

Fremont settled. He collected his cool, once more adjusted his cuffs. "You were seen making threats against the Councilman on national television, and now he's dead. All it takes is one anonymous phone call from us to say where the body is and you'll be on the hot seat for it."

"They'd have to make a case, prove I did it."

"Oh, they'll have proof alright. See it was your gun did the deed."

"My gun?"

Lougie looked up for the first time. He said, "From your nightstand."

Nuccio threw him a glance and Lougie went back to studying the lines in his palm.

"That's right!" Fremont continued. "And that very gun will be found with the body, your fingerprints all over it."

Thus far, Nuccio had been observing them with an air of calm amusement, now his face changed, his eyes narrowed, a vein at his temple began to pulse. "What is it you want?"

"We got you by the balls," Fremont said, "and we want some cash. Fifty…no…make that seventy-five thousand."

Nuccio pushed back in his chair and stood. His eyes ran from Fremont to Lougie. "Let me get this straight," Nuccio said. He turned to pace several steps away, seeming to think about it before turning again. "You broke into my private quarters to steal my gun, so you could use it to kill Hornackey, make it look like was me who did it. Now you want money to keep it quiet. Am I understanding this right?"

Fremont returned Nuccio's gaze without comment.

"What happens I pay you the money and the body shows up anyway? I'm still in deep shit."

"Cause once you give us the cash, we tell you where the body is, you can dispose of it your own way, recover the gun, toss it in the river, whatever. Don't guys like you have one of those *Cleaning Crews*?"

"Cleaning crew," Nuccio said, making sure he heard it correctly.

"Yeah, like in the movies, man," Fremont said. "Team comes in, disposes of the body, cleans up the blood, the prints, tosses the evidence."

"Oh, yeah, Cleaning Crew," Nuccio said.

"Either way, you'll know where the gun and the body is and can do your own thing with it, eliminate the evidence."

"And what if I decide, instead, to just cap the two of you right here? No phone calls to the authorities, life goes on."

Fremont turned to Lougie giving him a nudge on the shoulder. "Man says he's thinking of popping the two of us instead." Lougie gave-up an oafish laugh, but he sat up straight to pay attention now.

Turning back to Nuccio, Fremont said, "You could do that, sure, have the two of us popped. But run the risk of the body being found on its own, accidentally."

Nuccio rubbed his chin, giving the situation some thought. Then to Fremont, said, "One time, seventy-five thou? You tell me where the body's hidden and I don't see you guys ever again?"

"Like ghosts in the night, we'll be gone. Look at it as a business transaction. You didn't like the do-good Councilman, he was getting in the way of your land development projects, so we simply took care of a sticky problem for you. Consider it payment for services rendered."

There was a long dry moment between them, Nuccio holding Fremont's gaze. Fremont wasn't sure how much longer he could keep it together. Coming back at the man, eye to eye, but inside beginning to unravel. Finally, Nuccio nodded. "Services rendered, sure, why not."

Fremont let himself breath a little as Nuccio returned to his seat and fished a bulky paper sack from the desk drawer. From it, he dumped banded bundles of money onto the desk—lots of it. Fremont exchanged a glance with Lougie, the two of them wide-eyed, awed by the availability of so much cash.

"Money I tried to bride the Councilman with. Choirboy wouldn't take it," Nuccio said. "So, what the hell, now I'll give you some instead. Job's done either way, am I right?"

Nuccio began counting out stacks, a thousand at a time. Meanwhile, Fremont sat watching the monitors: a cement truck dispensing Ready mix into a pre-formed trench, workers guiding the gravely muck down the chute; a crane lowering banded stacks of lumber onto an upper platform; a man on a scaffold, in a welding helmet, connecting rebar amid a shower of sparkly fireworks.

"Seventy-five thousand," Nuccio said, finishing the count. He lifted the stack of bills, delicately, as if it were timed to go off, and sat it on the corner of the desk. "You can have it when you tell me where you placed the body."

Fremont could feel his mouth watering, the sight of all that cash so close. He stole a quick glance at Lougie, who seemed to be hypnotized by all that green. Fremont cleared his throat. "Alright. We dumped the body in the landfill, tossed the gun in with it."

Fremont was looking at Nuccio, the man's face changing now.

"The landfill?" Nuccio said, surprise showing, or maybe he hadn't heard right.

"Yeah, out on Lowfork Road," Fremont said.

Nuccio's face changed again. This time a slow grin worked its way across. He began taking money from the proffered stack and returning it to the paper sack. One by one the bundles disappeared before Fremont's eyes.

"Man, what are you doing? I thought we had a deal!"

"Does this mean we don't get paid?" Lougie asked.

Nuccio said nothing until all the money was retrieved, and the sack securely tucked away inside the desk drawer.

"I'm ready to cut a new deal," Nuccio said.

"New...I don't get it. Man, don't make me notify the police."

"Go ahead, make the call," Nuccio said. "While we're waiting for them to arrive we can watch some of my favorite home movies."

Fremont and Lougie exchanged questioning looks, as Nuccio keyed entries into his computer.

"When did you drop the body, was it last night?"

When there was no response, Nuccio continued. "I'm guessing midnight or so..." He tapped a few more keys then turned his attention to the monitors.

Across the bank of monitors the landfill appeared in various angled views. The nightscape was filled with rich illumination from the flood lamps, the pit and the barren land pack could be seen. Within seconds, Fremont's beat-up Monte Carlo came into view on one of the screens, and passed from monitor to monitor as it crossed the barren land pack.

"Bingo!" Nuccio said.

Fremont and Lougie watched themselves on video as they dispatched the Councilman from the trunk. One monitor captured them in profile, another full facial, while others documented them wide-angle. There was the debate over killing Hornackey, unheard, then the Councilman's attempted escape. The silent film unfolded as it had the night before: the flash from the revolver, the puff of smoke, the Councilman doubling to the ground.

"Not a bad shot," Nuccio said.

Fremont and Lougie sat mute, mouths open, as they watched themselves dump the body into the pit and toss the gun in with it.

Nuccio said, "Very compelling evidence, wouldn't you say? Didn't you boys catch the 'private' sign that read 'White Horse Development?'" Nuccio paused to enjoy the look on both their faces. "Well, it is a small sign I guess."

"Man, who video tapes a trash dump?" Fremont said, his face numb, feeling sick to his stomach.

"Gypsy dumpers were polluting my fill," Nuccio said. "Like you said, I'm a careful man."

Fremont sat fighting his nausea and trying to regain strength in his legs that had suddenly gone weak. Lougie had come to the edge of his seat; he seemed unable to draw his eyes from the monitors.

"You gonna turn us in?" Fremont asked. His voice was a little shaky.

Nuccio drew a cigar from his lap drawer. Striking fire to it and drawing heartily, he said, "Turn you in? What good would that do? Besides, you boys have done me a favor. That little zoning problem for my Crosstown Project has just gone away."

Nuccio leaned back in his chair, propped his feet on the desk, once again, and drew on his cigar.

"I'm thinking," he said, "maybe you two fuck-ups could be of some use to me."

"You mean, like a job?" Lougie asked.

"Yeah, call it a job. You understand, as long as I have the video, you'll have to do whatever I say."

"You want us to work for you," Fremont said, wanting to be sure.

"You want to look at it that way."

Fremont cheered to the idea. "Hey, shit, no problem. We could carry your bag money, serve as bodyguards, throw some muscle around when you need it." He winked. "Maybe even eliminate some of the competition it gets too stiff."

"Actually I had something else in mind."

"Sure, anything," Fremont said. "You're the boss. What do you have in mind?"

"I'm thinking about what you said about having a Cleaning Crew."

"Yeah, course. Cleaning Crew. First job, got a body out there needs to be disposed of."

"Actually…" Nuccio said. He drew on his cigar and blew smoke at the ceiling, watched it as it swirled and dissipated. "…I was thinking you could start with the floors. The mop closet's down the hall."

RUNNING IN PLACE

Maggie Rogers was moving fast, faster than was safe, she knew, weaving in and out of traffic heading south. She'd put more than three hundred miles between her and the last town she'd spent the night in. Still, she couldn't take her eyes off the rearview mirror, nor take the one hand off the gun she held cradled in her lap. No sign of him yet, she thought. No sign of his black SUV, the steely-eyed Ram emblem bearing down fast. No sign of her husband, Boone.

She had passed through Lexington, Kentucky more than half an hour ago. Dusk was setting in; it would be dark soon. Perhaps, under the cover of darkness, she could change direction again, double back on her tracks and head west once more. Would it matter? Probably not. Boone would find her, she was sure of it.

Maggie watched the rearview mirror. One after another, cars fell in her wake and disappeared behind her—RVs, boat trailers, trucks, SUVs. All except one.

There had been a dark shape in the rear distance for some time now. It was large. Was it black? Could the dark shape be Boone?

Near midnight, she reached the Tennessee state line. The town of Jellico lay just ahead. The black shape—or what she believed to be its headlights now—was still back there in the distance. Or perhaps not. Maybe it was some other car or truck that had mixed and merged with the changing traffic. Perhaps Boone had not followed her at all. Wasn't that a reasonable possibility? No—not with Boone. *"You ever try to leave me, girl, I'll kill you! I swear to God!"* Boone had told her once during a heated argument. And he would. Boone would never let her go, not without a showdown; Boone would never let her go—*period*.

Cresting a rise, she could see lighted signs ahead—gas stations, fast food restaurants, motels—the town of Jellico lying mostly in the gap to the right side of the Interstate. She was low on gas. But could she risk making a stop?

The vehicle back there in the distance, maybe Boone, the exit ramp approaching fast—Maggie had a decision to make.

She checked the mirror again. The headlights she believed to be the SUV were gone, disappeared beyond the rise.

Maggie cut the wheel hard to the right. The car dove off the exit, picking up speed down hill. She killed her lights and let the car run free in darkness. At the bottom of the ramp, she fought the urge to apply the brakes, fearing the flash of light would give her away. Instead, she checked quickly for cross traffic and powered the car left onto the crossroad without stopping for the sign.

Maggie sped the car beneath the overpass away from the main collection of business establishments. On the far side of the Interstate, she jacked the car off the road and into the parking lot of a rundown motel. It was largely unpopulated on this side of the highway—dark, but for a porch light above the motel office door and the red neon *vacancy* sign. The motel itself was no more than a string of doors along a brick front. Maggie wheeled the car into the shadows beyond the last unit.

In the dark, the engine idling, Maggie lifted the gun from her lap and cradled it close. Cocking the hammer, she watched the mirror closely. Headlights appeared on the exit ramp…

Boone—his jealousy had driven them apart. Maggie was barely twenty years old this day, but they had been married…*How long was it now?* It seemed she couldn't remember a time when they weren't.

She could remember a time when he had not been so possessive. A time before they'd first become intimate. That time seemed long ago, but probably wasn't.

She'd dropped out of school to be Boone's wife. Boone had insisted. Beginning then and continuing, Boone had opposed her freedom: first with firm protestations, then, as her need for independence deepened, with rage. "Slut! Whore!" he'd call her—times she'd try to leave the house.

In time, Maggie found herself with no friends, and no contact beyond the walls of their house. Boone owned Maggie, pure and simple. Boone would never let her go.

The headlights drew to a stop at the bottom of the exit ramp. There it sat, idling, as if the driver were trying to decide what to do next—a black SUV. "God, don't let it be Boone," Maggie prayed.

Slowly the vehicle moved, turning right away from her and toward the populated side of the freeway. Seeing its taillights disappear along the strip, Maggie let her breath out and eased the hammer down on the revolver. Sitting there in the darkness, Maggie began to cry…

The events of the last evening seemed muddled. All her nights of late seemed muddled. Memories passed in vaporous clouds, like seeing her past projected onto a moving bank of fog. She could conjure images, but not discern the background; recall events, but with no correlation to place or time. Had Boone caught up to her the previous night?…no, why would she think that?

"You dirty slut! Who is he, Maggie? Or's there more than one? Maybe you're sleeping with all of them."

She could hear voices, loud when they came to her.

"Boone, you're hurting me!"

Contents of her handbag scattered on the floor.

Was that in their home in Mobile? Or the motel room in Lafayette? Why was it so hard to remember?

"Keep your hands off me, Boone!"

A table overturning; a lamp breaking.

"Slut!

A cloud of dust in her review mirror, a glimpse of Boone charging from the porch.

Had he caught up to her that time?

"Where the hell you think you're going, girl?"

A hard knock on the window…

Another…

Maggie jolted into the present to find a man, standing with a bucket of ice beside the car. He was poised to knock again. Seeing Maggie with the gun he backed a step away.

"Hold on," he said, his voice calm. "I don't mean no harm."

Maggie lowered the gun and powered the window down. "I'm sorry," she said.

The man continued to watch her closely. "Are you okay?"

Maggie nodded yes, then said, "No."

The man observed her for a moment longer. "Listen, I know you don't know me, but I was just about to fix myself a drink. Maybe you could use one. Mine's the end unit right here."

Maggie nodded, but turned in her seat to scan the highway beyond the overpass.

"There's no one there," the man assured her. "You'll be alright with me."

Avery Johnson was fifty years old, but not bad looking, dressed in work pants and a plaid cotton shirt. The room was shabby and undignified. But the bedding was clean, and the bathroom had been recently remodeled. Still, Avery Johnson apologized for the untidiness.

They sat with the door closed, sipping Jack Daniel's over ice. The man told her he was from Danville, Illinois, here on business, calling on farm stores to sell his company's fertilizers. Maggie told him maybe she would go on to Mobile in the morning. She'd grown up there.

"I've got a wife and a daughter and a newly arrived grandchild, one month old," Avery told her. "What about you? You married?"

"No…wait…yes…I can't remember," Maggie said.

It drew a look of discernment, but Maggie followed quickly with, "I'm not now…or might not be soon…I don't know. I'm thinking I'll visit my sister, Iris. If she'll take me in."

"In Mobile?" the man said.

"In Manchester…no, right…in Mobile."

The whiskey tasted good. And for a time Maggie forgot that Boone might be out there, prowling the night looking for her, forgot that Boone would kill them both if he caught them here together, whiskey glasses in their hands.

Avery Johnson didn't ask why she was on the run; didn't question when she sometimes became confused. He was a nice man. And Maggie liked the way he looked.

She liked the way he looked at her also. It was with a certain appreciation, she couldn't ever remember getting from Boone. Not lewd, but with a sense that she was female and pretty, and he was male and in need. And later, when he came around to stand behind her chair and stroke her neck, she let him. Let him because it felt good and she needed to feel something just now. Feel anything that would penetrate the numbness of her life and let her just…be.

And so, she didn't remove his hand when it slipped inside her blouse. And she didn't object when he led her to the bed. And she didn't hold back—crying out—when she made love astride his hips. And didn't move for long hours afterward, until all the tremors had been stilled.

Maggie didn't wait for daylight. She left the stranger on the bed, slipping into pre-morning darkness, and pointed her car south again. Boone had not found her. Not yet. But it wasn't good to stay in one place too long. Besides, if she was ever going to be free of Boone, she had to make it to Mobile and Iris'. In the entire history of her marriage to him, sister Iris was the only one who could handle Boone. She was the only one who seemed to *have his number* and with a word be able to put him in his place. Iris would protect her…or should protect her…or…it was becoming confused again.

By late morning, Maggie began to think, perhaps, she'd shaken Boone's tail. She was tired of driving, tired of running, and tired of feeling afraid.

In a gas station, north of Huntsville, Maggie met a young man who said he was trying to get to Selma. He helped her pump the gas, and when it was done and paid for, Maggie offered him a ride.

They passed through farmland that looked like it hadn't seen rain in a while—tomatoes wilted on the vine and corn that had dried in the shuck. They talked, only a little. The seemingly shy young man rode with his eyes glued to the passing fields.

Maggie studied the man—a boy really. He was handsome, had a nice, easy smile, and wore his shaggy hair in a casual way, down across his forehead. He sat with a kind of carefree slouch, his hip cocked slightly her way. His jeans and dark, knit shirt fit loose, but she could tell he was lean and strong.

He would turn occasionally to find her looking at him, and Maggie would look away. The road slipped behind them. And Maggie thought…*interesting,* how the road, trailing away behind the car, might be viewed as a metaphor for life. The patch of road in front of the car became the patch of road behind it. What was here became instantly there. What was now became then. What happened to those patches of road, she wondered? Did they remain in place and time, or once passed, did they mix and muddle, as her memory often did.

And so, when the image of Boone came into her mind, she cast it out. And when the young man caught her looking again, she didn't turn away. And when they found a road—a set of tractor ruts running off into the fields—Maggie pulled the car to a place beneath the dried stalks of corn and gave herself up to the young man with abandon. Only when they were done, did the dark shadow of Boone return.

It was late afternoon when Maggie finally reached Mobile. Iris lived in the house on Canter Street. The same house the two of them had grown up in. Amazingly, it had gone unchanged: the same white aluminum siding, the same windowed gables above the porch, the same untended patches of weeds in the yard. How long had it been since she'd last been here? A week? A year?

Maggie climbed the front steps and rang the bell.

There was no answer right away. Then, as Maggie was about to ring again, the door opened. Iris stood looking down at her, her bony frame squared in the doorway.

It took Maggie a second to reconcile her sister's looks. She was…what?…three years older? Maggie had to think. Maggie was twenty, which would make Iris twenty-three. But this woman in the doorway before her clearly wore the look of time. Her cheeks were sunken and there were deep lines cutting crows feet at the corners of her eyes. She was much thinner than Maggie remembered. Still, it was Iris. It was.

"It's me, Maggie," Maggie said into an unmoving face.

"Maggie," Iris said curtly. "I didn't think I'd ever see you again." Iris observed her for a moment, then said, "But, I guess you're here, aren't you? Come in." She held the door for Maggie to pass.

They took seats in the living room. Maggie eased onto the divan, sat with her hands clasped in her lap, while Iris perched on the edge of a chair opposite her. Maggie took a moment to look around. The inside of the house was unchanged too: same Early American furniture, same white lace doilies, same knitted afghans, same sundial clock above the mantle.

"The place looks good," Maggie said.

Iris remained stone-faced, observing her coldly.

"I didn't know where else to go," Maggie said. "Boone is after me again. I'm scared he's going to do something real bad this time."

"Boone?" Iris said.

"You know what a temper he has."

Iris appraised her closely before saying. "You look tired, dear."

"I drove most of the night to get here."

Iris rose, gathering an afghan off the back of the chair, and crossed around the coffee table to where Maggie sat. "I'm sure we have things to talk about," Iris said. "But why don't we save it until you've had a rest."

Iris eased Maggie down onto the sofa, covering her with the Afghan.

"I am tired," Maggie said, giving in to the comfort of the knitted coverlet. Somewhere outside, a car's engine revved and Maggie came upright once more.

"It's all right, dear," Iris said. "It's just a car on the street."

"But it might be, Boone!"

"I'll make sure it's not," Iris said, easing Maggie down again and stroking her hair to calm her.

Maggie allowed herself to be cooed and slowly drifted into sleep, where her dreams came without rhythm or rhyme.

Maggie awoke to the sound of another vehicle. She bolted from her place on the sofa and peered through the window. A black SUV sat parked in the driveway alongside the house.

She raced back to the sofa to retrieve her purse. Hurriedly she fished inside for the gun...a billfold...keys...lipstick, Kleenex, Chapstick...

There was no revolver.

"Looking for this?" she heard Iris say.

Maggie turned to see Iris with the gun in her hand. It was pointed in Maggie's direction.

"Boone! That's Boone out there!" Maggie said.

The doorbell rang.

"Just stay put, Maggie."

"God, Iris, don't let him in!"

Iris called to the entrance. "The door's open! Come in!"

"Iris, no!"

Maggie wanted to run, flee the house she'd grown up in. But terror, in heavy slabs, held her feet to the floor.

At the doorway to the living room, a tall and formidable figure appeared. But instead of the cruel and rage filled face of Boone, the face in the doorway looked sympathetic. "Maggie," he said, by way of greeting.

Iris crossed quickly to the man and handed him the revolver. She said, "Maggie, this is Daniel Riker, he's a U.S. Marshal."

"But that's Boone's vehicle, the SUV, in the driveway, he's been chasing me. He'll kill me if he finds me."

"That's my vehicle, Maggie," Marshal Riker said. "I thought I almost caught up with you coming out of Kentucky. But somehow you gave me the slip. I've been following the trail of bodies you've left across six states."

"Bodies?" Maggie shook her head. "I don't understand. What bodies?"

"Seven that we've counted," the U.S. Marshal said. "There was the gas station attendant in Arkansas, a jogger in Missouri. The latest was a fertilizer salesman, we found in a motel in Tennessee, and what we believed to be a drifter, a hitch-hiker, in a cornfield near Huntsville. All killed with the same gun, Maggie." Riker dangled the revolver by the grip, for her to see.

Maggie eyed Riker, trying to puzzle it, trying to piece things together. The gun...bodies...there were how many states?...how many nights?....

Things were starting to get muddled again.

...a hitchhiker...Was that last week?...there was a motel in...Where?...

"What about my husband, Boone?" Maggie said. "Haven't you tried to locate him? It's his gun. Ask my sister! Iris, tell him! It's Boone!"

Iris and the Marshal shared a guarded look. After a moment, Iris said, "Mag-gie..." she hesitated, seeming to search her mind carefully for the right words to say. "It's Boone's gun all right. But I'm not your sister...I'm your mother. And Boone is not your husband. He's your father. Or was until you shot him where he slept, eight nights ago."

"But..." *her father*, Maggie thought.

Boone was her husband. She could remember intimacies. She could. Boone coming to her bed at night...no, wait, Boone belonged to Iris'...Iris kept Boone in his place...Why would she think that? No! There had been a wedding party the night she turned sixteen...she remembered that very clearly because...wait...a birthday party seemed more right...but then why had Boone?...

Maggie felt a touch. She looked to find the Marshal, the man Iris called Daniel Riker, at her elbow. "Come on, Maggie," he said. His touch was gentle and compassionate as he led her toward the door.

Maggie looked back across her shoulder to see Iris, her arms hugged tightly beneath her breasts, tears welling in her eyes. "Goodbye, Mommy," Maggie said, though the words sounded strange to her ears.

And to the Marshal, as he lead her out, she said, "You won't let Boone get me, will you?"

Running In Place was the winner of the 2004 Fire To Fly Competition.

A MIRACLE FOR FATHER VEGA

There were souls to be saved. Father Emilio Vega had to remind himself of that as he finished loading the rickety wooden wheelbarrow with loose sand and rock. The desert sun was blistering and he would need to drink soon. But first he would finish this load.

Bracing his back for the task, Emilio got a firm grip on the handles. He got the wheelbarrow started, feeling his knees wobble. There were holes to be filled. A brace of some sort would be advisable, he knew. A hernia, and this important work would go undone.

Up the rise and onto the desert floor, Emilio navigated the heavy load through dense desert scrub. Sandals flapping, his short, fat legs churned to keep the weight moving. Sweat dripped from his forehead and soaked the handkerchief tied to protect his balding scalp from the sun. His faded cassock—the one he wore sometimes over jockeys, but today was worn over nothing at all—it too was soaked.

He chose his path carefully, watching to avoid the areas where red flags—flags he had placed himself—warned of danger. The desert was pocked with holes—dozens, maybe hundreds of them—mineshafts left abandoned decades ago. A few were open and could be spotted. Others had been boarded over sometime in the past and covered with sand. A stupid thing. Now the boards beneath the sand were rotted and riddled with termites and hidden. A false step and he could be sent through rotting timbers to a near bottomless grave.

Emilio tipped his load into one of the marked shafts and jostled the wheelbarrow empty. Straightening, biting off the pain that seared his back, Emilio turned his eyes to his beloved church. There in the desert, so blessed it was. A crumbling adobe structure, stalwart, amid the scrub. There was divine purpose to the draining labor, Emilio told himself. The holes must be filled for the safety of others. The Virgin herself had instructed him so.

Emilio heard a rumble in the distance and looked out to the gravel road leading up to the church. A vehicle approached fast, trailed by a cloud of dust. *Madre de Dios.* One more thing to deal with, he thought.

Emilio removed his handkerchief and used it to mop the sweat and desert grime from his face. Then, with a quick sign of the cross and a glance toward God, he started the trek back to the church, careful to avoid the flags.

When Emilio reached the entrance, he found the vehicle, a full-sized pick-up truck, parked in front. It was a late model, covered in dust. The driver was nowhere in sight. Emilio crossed to the doorway of the church and stepped inside. The truck's owner, a man, was standing hands on hip in the center aisle, gazing up at the tall statue of the Virgin Mary.

"Can I help you?" Emilio asked.

The man dropped his hands and turned.

"You people sure like your symbolism," he said. He was dressed in work boots and a work coverall. The sleeves of the coverall were rolled to reveal thick forearms. The zipper was zipped only halfway up the chest to reveal a mass of dark hair. He was Caucasian, American likely, hard and rough looking. A worker, perhaps, from the copper mines to the south. But something in the man's tone, his demeanor, tripped warnings inside Emilio's head.

He had seen men like this one before—gringos from north of the border who came to work the mines. You could see them brawling outside the cantinas on Friday nights, or dragging rolls of chicken wire with their trucks through the center of town, just to stir up dust and intimidate the locals. Wild animals.

Emilio said, "Yes, of course, it is part of our culture, our beliefs. Are you not Catholic?"

"To tell the truth, Padre, this is the first time I've ever been inside one of your churches. It could use a coat of paint, you know it?"

"Are you a painting contractor?" Emilio asked.

The man came forward now, to stand face to face.

"Naw! I guess I've done my share of labor, but I'm more into the management end of business these days. But speaking of work, I've got to say, Padre, you look like you've been around the field a few times yourself." The man reached out to finger Emilio's dirty cassock, fuss at a patch of dirt on his shoulder.

"I am trying to refill the holes," Emilio said.

"Holes? What holes would that be?"

"The abandoned shafts," Emilio said. "The ones left over from the old days, when wildcat prospectors would pick a spot in the desert and begin digging. They are empty, now, and many are boarded over. They pose a great danger to my congregation."

The man seemed to consider this, but said, "Listen, Padre, why don't you take a seat?"

Emilio observed the man for a moment, the directed warning that seemed to reside just behind the man's eyes, then slipped into the last pew along the aisle. When he was seated, he said, "Yes, what is it? What business do you have with the church?"

The man did not sit, but rather chose to remain on his feet, leaning over Emilio, close to his face. Emilio thought he detected a hint of alcohol, tequila he imagined—eleven thirty in the morning—mixed with the man's sweat. He waited, for the man to speak.

"Tell me, Padre, how are you fixed for insurance?"

"Insurance?" Emilio said, trying to puzzle the reason for the question. "The church is made of adobe clay, there is little to insure, little of value."

"No, see, what I'm thinking, Padre, is personal injury insurance."

A light went on in Emilio's head. He had heard stories in town of the man named Cole Safford. A man who had once been in the employ of the big mines, but who was now known for running roughshod over the locals and terrorizing their businesses. That man had been pointed out to him once on the main street of town. Emilio was sure this man was one and the same. He was called "*Saff*" by his cronies, he recalled.

It was told that the man made his living by soliciting money from business owners. If they didn't pay, their business would mysteriously burn to the ground in the middle of the night. Protection money, Emilio had heard it called. The man had his boys—other American roughneck miners to help him carry out the threats.

In the confessional, members of his congregation had spoken of their shame and fear of this man. He had taken the women of the village against their will, often the wives of poor farmers or shopkeepers. He brutalized the men, sometimes relieving them of their meager wages before they could reach home with it.

And he intimidated or paid off local authorities to turn their eyes the other way. Emilio said, "You want me to pay you, so you will not hurt me?"

"Now, Padre, how would that look in the eyes of God, assaulting a priest? No, I wasn't so much thinking of you personally, as your flock. All those businesses out there...you've seen them along the market place, down the main street of town...they all pay me to make sure their assets are protected. I figure your greatest asset is your congregation. I'm sure you wouldn't want things to start happening to your flock that would prevent them from coming to Mass each Sunday."

Emilio dizzied, but he held it together. He said, "Yes, and are you not worried about what God's eyes would think of that?"

"Well, I've never been what you call religious. But I have to say, I do admire your trappings...all the crosses, the pretty statues, the little wafers and wine, supposed to be the flesh and blood of Jesus. It makes for interesting conversation, Padre."

"How am I, in good faith," Emilio said, "supposed to face God and tell him that I let you take money from His church? Money given from the hearts of His followers to further His name."

"Well, I'm sure the two of you are on close speaking terms, Padre. I'll let you work it out with Him." Saff straightened and took a toothpick from the breast pocket of his coverall. He slipped it into the corner of his mouth. "I'll be back Monday, Padre, following Sunday's services. Be sure to have your payment ready. Let's say, oh...half the offering. How's that? That should be enough to insure the well being of your congregation."

Saff let the toothpick slide across his mouth. He studied Emilio for a moment, then turned and left the church.

Emilio watched the man go, measured the swagger in his stride as he pushed out the door. He heard the truck outside start up. Then heard the crunching of gravel beneath its tires as it made the turn-around and departed.

Emilio sat calming his nerves. He thought of God and the work He had given him. And he thought of Job in the Bible. God had placed obstacles, one after the other, in Job's way, as a way to test his faith. Perhaps this was a test. Perhaps not. Either way, Emilio decided, Job knew little of gangsters who extort money from the church. And little more about all the holes that needed to be filled.

*   *   *   *

Building his dream had been difficult. Attendance for Mass was usually modest at best. Among the congregation, there were a few shop owners and a handful of workers from the mines. But mostly his flock consisted of poor villagers, simple people, with little to spare. After a year of passing out flyers in the marketplace and visiting the townspeople in their homes, the church refused to grow. It stagnated with no more than twenty-five to thirty weekly attendees. His vision for his little fixer-upper church in the desert was that of the magnificent San Xavier Del Bac mission he had visited once, north and across the border in Arizona. The old, refurbished mission was called the "Dove of the Desert" for its peace and its beauty. By comparison, his little church, on the outskirts of Obregon Ciudad, might well be labeled the "Pigeon of the Plains." It was in such need of repair. A coat of whitewash would at least brighten its presence on the landscape. And the leaky roof needed to be fixed. But there were limited funds to hire the work done, and with attendance modest, the offerings remained low. Emilio had heard this type of situation referred to as a Catch-22. To grow the offerings to afford the repairs, he had to build attendance. To attract more attendees he had to make the repairs and beautify the church. Such a dilemma.

Over the past year, Emilio prayed nightly and again each morning. "Please, God, show me the way," he would say. But nothing.

For the longest time, it went on that way—Emilio wearing the skin off his knees in prayer, while God was apparently off somewhere playing golf…then, one morning, his prayers were answered.

The *Virgin* had appeared only recently in the smooth green bark of the Palo Verde tree—the one off in the desert, beyond the church, on the small sloping hillside some one-hundred-yards away. It had not been there before; Father Vega was sure of this. But there she was now, the image of her as clear as could be. Her tears flowed in sap down the trunk of the tree. They dripped to the dry barren sand, where a single cactus flower had bloomed. She was beautiful in her sorrow.

It *was* a Miracle, Emilio knew, sent by God. And it was God's answer to his prayers. If the miracle should be revealed, believers far and wide would be drawn to the little church in the desert, where the Virgin herself offered the message of hope and salvation for all to see. It was a reversal of the Catch-22, Emilio realized—people would come, the offerings would grow, repairs and the long awaited beautification of the church could be implemented. Thus, even more people would be inspired to come. Truly a miracle of God.

*   *   *   *

Sunday's offering was modest—sixty-eight pesos—to be split with the man called Saff. There would be little left to advance the dream. Monday morning,

Emilio was back at work, hauling sand and rock from the wash to fill the holes. It was an impossible task. So many holes, *Madre de Dios*, and so little help to fill them. If God had given him the answer to his prayers, Emilio considered, why then would He place such an obstacle as the man, Saff, to impede his progress in restoring the church? Sometimes God was difficult to figure, Emilio thought. Sometimes God didn't make sense.

At noon, Emilio broke from his labors to have lunch and consider what to do about Saff. He would be coming this afternoon, expecting to be paid. He filled his belly with beans and rice, and thanked God for the Miracle that would help him build his church. But he added a footnote, imploring, "What should I do, Lord? What should I do about this man who has come to take what little we have? Tell me. Will you intervene? Or are you looking for me to solve this alone?"

Sitting in the shade of the porch outside his one room rectory, Emilio sat with a jar of water looking out across the desert scrub dotted with warning flags, and to the tree on the hillside beyond. He thought of the Miracle, its appearance. And of the Virgin herself, waiting out there for the chance to deliver her message. He had asked God for an answer. "Should I turn over the money and keep working, Lord? Is that what you want? Or do I refuse? But if I refuse, how do you expect me to stand by and watch members of my congregation selectively terrorized? How can I face them with a quiet heart in confessional?"

Emilio thought he'd heard an answer amid his prayers. But, had it truly been the voice of God offering a solution? Or had it only been his own thoughts and ideas, ricocheting around inside his head? Emilio looked off down the gravel road toward the city? "So, what's it going to be?" Emilio asked himself. "Do you roll over for this man, or not?"

*   *   *   *

Shortly after two o'clock the truck appeared on the gravel road, followed by the customary cloud of dust. From the doorway, Emilio watched as it made its way into the turnaround at the front of the church.

The man, Saff, killed the engine and stepped out, his eyes cast out across the desert, observing the red flags.

Approaching, he said, "Holes. Those the holes you were talking about?"

Emilio nodded. "The flags mark the spots. The ones I know of."

The man seemed to consider the idea. Then said, "So, Padre, were you able to explain things to God and still keep your job?"

"I spoke to him, yes," Emilio said.

"Yea, what'd he say?"

"God said it is the job of the shepherd to protect his flock."

"Sounds like a right smart God at that," Saff said. "So you have money for me."

"I have it," Emilio said. He brought a small paper bag from the pocket of his robe and offered it to Saff. "Half the Sunday offering, as you requested. It is all there."

Saff took the bag, shook it, and listened to it jingle. "You're a wise and honorable man, Padre. I thank you, and your congregation thanks you, all them sheep."

Saff turned to his truck. Emilio followed, as would be his habit of sending all visitors graciously on their way. He watched as Saff opened the door and tossed the sack of money in ahead of him. Emilio could see on the seat other bags and envelopes—dozens of them. Money from others he'd extorted. Emilio imagined Monday to be Saff's collection day—the man getting his work done early in the week, so he could drink beer in the cantina with his friends the rest of the time.

Saff hesitated before getting in, letting his eyes return to the flag dotted landscape. "You know, I have to ask one thing, Padre. How come you work so hard to fill those holes? Why not just throw up a barrier and some warning signs to keep people out?"

Emilio hesitated, then admitted, "It's for the Miracle. I'm repairing the land so the townspeople can witness the appearance of the blessed Virgin."

"The Virgin? No shit, you say!"

"Yes. There on the hillside, the Palo Verde tree, where she has appeared."

"Hell, I don't believe I've ever witnessed a miracle before, much less met a virgin. What's that like?"

"You can see for yourself," Emilio said. "All who cast eyes upon her will receive her grace. Their greatest prayers will be answered."

"She can get your prayers answered, can she, kinda like wishin' on a star?"

Emilio said nothing, but crossed back to the church. At the doorway he stopped. "Should you like to witness her, be very careful not to walk where you see the flags." And with that he went inside. It was time to call on God.

*   *   *   *

The following day, a car arrived from town, and the Police Commissioner from Obregon waved Emilio from the field where he was working to fill one of the holes, one nearest the hillside.

Emilio greeted the Commissioner—a small little Mexican with a pencil mustache and an ill-fitting suit—and asked what he could do for him this morning.

"I'm looking for someone, Father. A man named Cole Safford," the little policeman said. "His friends said he had plans to come out to the church yesterday afternoon, and hasn't been seen or heard from since."

"Yes, the man Saff, he was here," Emilio said.

"So, he did come?"

"Yes, he came. We talked about God's wishes and about the blessed Virgin, then I assume he returned to the city."

"Assume," the little policeman said, a hint of suspicion in his voice.

"Yes. I left him beside his car to go prepare the sacrament. And, as you can see, his car is no longer here."

The little policeman surveyed the area casually, then said, "So you're still trying to fill the old mine shafts alone, Father?"

"Yes, I do it alone for now," Emilio said. "But I believe help is on the way."

"Yeah, well, some say you're just plain loco, Father. But if it's what you wish to do."

"It is what God wishes," Emilio said.

"Uh-huh," the policeman said. "Well, listen…if you should hear from this man Saff again, tell him his friends are concerned for him."

"I will be sure to tell him the very next time I see him," Emilio said. "I promise."

Emilio watched until the Commissioner's car was down the road and gone, then crossed back through the desert scrub to the hole near the hillside, beneath the Virgin's sorrowful gaze.

He peered into the deep, gaping hole with the shattered wooden rim, to the fresh pile of sand and rock down there a great distance. "Your friends are looking for you, Señor Safford," he said into the hole, fulfilling his promise. Then he turned his eyes to the Virgin, who seemed to have abandoned her soulful gaze for that of a smile this morning.

"God has blessed us, Madre," he told the image. "The money on the seat of the truck will surely fund laborers to fill the remaining shafts and perhaps repair the leaky roof. Then I can invite the masses to see you. It will be soon. You'll see."

Emilio glanced off toward the skyline. "Still there is much work to do first," he said, more to himself than to the image. "I will need to find a deep canyon off the road in which to dump the car. And, of course…I must return the flags to their proper places."

ONLY IN THE MOVIES

The woman's voice was sultry, almost a whisper, when she asked Gallow to meet her at Vincenti's. "It's on Sunset. Do you know it?" she said.

It had been a while, maybe six months, since Gallow had been close to a woman—well, in an intimate way—and the soft voice stirred familiar longings in places he realized he'd been neglecting. "How's eight-thirty sound?"

"Ask Gar for Olivia," the woman said, and ended the call.

Gar, it turned out, was a collapsible little matri'd too short to ride the rides at Disney. He led Gallow through a libidinous atmosphere, past checkered table cloths and Tiffany hanging lamps, to a booth at the back of the restaurant.

"Madam, a Mister Gallow to see you," Gar said and then was gone.

Gallow said, "You're the woman who called?"

She was dressed in black, with a long scarf wrapped once about her neck. The ends were tossed with flair over her shoulders. She seemed to study Gallow, smoking casually without regard for rules or patrons.

Gallow studied her back. "Can you actually see through those things in here?"

"I prefer to remain incognito," the woman said.

A waiter appeared. Gallow said, "Beer...whatever you've got on tap, and you might as well bring her another of whatever she's drinking." Watching the woman watch him, he said, "Do I know you? You look familiar?"

The woman tipped her glasses to the end of her nose, letting herself come out from behind them momentarily. She looked directly at Gallow, with gray-green eyes and said, "I don't know. Do you?"

She let the glasses perch there long enough for Gallow to get a good look. He said, "Yeah…you're that…that…movie star…what's her name … Doris … no … Dorothy … Dorothy Lamont, am I right?"

Using one manicured finger to tip the glasses back in place, she said, "I go by Olivia Hostetter in public."

Gallow couldn't help but notice her hands. She had exceptionally long, slender fingers, the nails done to perfection. Her skin was flawless.

"You were in that movie *Cape Destiny*. What a great picture. You played the woman who discovered her husband was a serial killer, and had to live with him while you set him up to be caught. I remember you almost got killed yourself near the end. Very thrilling scene, you don't mind my saying."

She looked off, the cigarette still poised. After a moment she took a quick drag and stubbed it out. "Yes, well, those days are behind me now."

Gallow couldn't seem to take his eyes off her. Okay—he had to admit—he was feeling a bit star struck. Here he was, no shit, across the booth, in touching distance of the great, the famous, Dorothy Lamont. How many movies had she made? The thriller, and one other he remembered, a period piece where she played the budding young daughter of a Russian Czar, and falling prey to Rasputin, Rumplestiltskin, whatever the hairy guy's name was…God! He had hated that animal, the character sure, but the one who deflowered that tender beauty. Here, at the table, she was older, now, and hidden behind glasses, but in his mind he saw her as she'd appeared in that film—a translucent mixture of frail vulnerability and raw sexuality. A slender, Nicole Kidman type, who could make a male audience ache with longing for her. Jesus! Gallow thought.

Yeah, she was probably late forties now. But Gallow couldn't help wondering how much of that divine allure was still alive back there behind the dark glasses and beneath the loose clothing. At last, he said, "Ms. Lamont, you mind telling me why you called me here?"

"Olivia," she said, "always 'Olivia' in public."

There was no anger in her voice, just that same sultry softness that had stirred him over the phone. He watched her pull a manila envelope from her bag on the seat beside her and reach to lay it in front of him on the table.

"I need your services, Mister Gallow. I've been told you're the best."

The waiter arrived with the drinks and Gallow waited until he'd gone, before saying, "You obviously haven't talked to my ex-wife."

The woman gave him a bored look.

"All right," he said, "what is it you want me to do?"

"I believe my husband is having an affair," she said. "I want you to prove me right or prove me wrong. There's a picture of him in the envelope and information to help you get started. There's a separate envelope with ten thousand dollars cash. Is that enough to begin?"

Gallow tried to peer through the dark glasses to the woman's eyes, hoping to read something from them. When his attempt at x-ray vision failed, he took up the envelope and removed an eight-by-ten glossy, a headshot of the man she claimed to be her husband.

"You may have heard of him," Dorothy Lamont said. "Dino Giovanni. His birth name is actually Dean Johnson. He's a fashion designer."

"Does he do well at that?" Gallow asked.

She shrugged. "Okay, I guess. Though it seems Polish designers are all the rage right now. Go figure. He has this little faggot named Jonathan who actually creates the designs. Dino found him in Las Vegas doing some cheesy club act, but mostly sewing costumes for the showgirls on the side. He brought him to L.A., and with my husband's...or should I say *my* contacts in the entertainment industry...the two went into business, turning out originals for the red carpet set."

"Dino Giovanni, huh?" Gallow said, studying the photo. "Can't say I've heard of him. He looks like George Hamilton. Is he always that tan?"

"You kidding...the wavy haired sonofabitch...he's fifty-three, thinks he's twenty. He spends more time at the spa than I do. And that's no joke."

"What makes you think he's got someone on the side?" Gallow asked.

"Just intuition, I suppose. He seems to be working longer and longer hours. Sometimes he doesn't come home at all. He'll say, 'I slept on the sofa at the studio.' Or 'I had a little too much to drink, I got a room.' When he is home, he has very little interest in me I'm afraid. All I want is for you to keep an eye on him and tell me what you see."

"All right," Gallow said, slipping the photo back into the envelope, "I'll bite."

Gallow downed a healthy portion of his beer and slipped out of the booth. He turned to go, then hesitated and turned back. He felt foolish, but considered he'd maybe never get a better chance. He said, "I've always been a big fan of yours, Ms. Lamont...I mean...Olivia...I'm still a big fan. Do you suppose I could trouble you for an autograph? Just on the envelope perhaps."

The woman gave him a look of annoyance but turned to her bag to fish inside.

"Here, allow me," Gallow said, producing a pen from his coat pocket and offering it to her with the point already ejected. "Just say, 'To John.'"

She took it, scribbled her name quickly on the envelope, and handed both pen and envelope back with a gesture of finality.

Gallow looked it over. "Thanks, I know it's a silly thing, but it means a lot to me, really."

Olivia—Dorothy Lamont—looked away as though he were nothing more than an errand boy she'd instructed and dismissed. She pulled a cigarette from her purse, lit it and blew smoke off in the other direction. Gallow excused himself with a nod. She was the great Dorothy Lamont; he was a lowly Private Investigator—it put him only one rung up from 'bug' on her grand social ladder. But he considered himself lucky. Lucky to have met her.

The job of surveilling Dino Giovanni—or Dean Johnson, whichever you preferred—began the following morning. The information package Dorothy Lamont had given him was well prepared. In it was an extensive list of places Dino frequented, along with names and addresses of those with close association to the man. Gallow picked up the trail at the Giovanni studio. It was on Rodeo Drive, a half-block north of Wilshire. The studio itself was above the street and looked down through spacious windows onto other trendy shops and designer boutiques.

Gallow parked in a loading zone across the street and remained in the car. He had his coffee; he had his Krispy Creme doughnuts. From his position, he could see inside the studio, through the wide windows. It was a fishbowl with furnishings. There was a modern Lucite desk and chair near the window. And a seating arrangement comprised of a sofa and a pair of matching armchairs. Beyond all that—what Gallow could see—were filing cabinets, mannequins, and what he believed might be a light table for evaluating composites. Gallow guessed the openness was intentional—a celebrity designer wishing to see and be seen.

It was eight-thirty, morning, and there was already movement inside the studio. He could see a delicate, feminine, young man flitting about. Gallow pictured him as a hummingbird, popping from flower to flower. This would be Jonathan, he decided.

And there were a couple of young Bohemian girls in there with him—artsy types you might see hanging around Starbucks. Together, the three of them hustled here, bustled there, doing whatever it was that assistants to the designer might do. It was the routine of a work-a-day office that Gallow had no concept of. He'd spent six years in the Marine Corps, another eighteen with the LAPD, and had been on his own now for more than five years. All that nervous energy behind the glass seemed pointless to him.

Gallow sipped his coffee and watched both the studio and the street surrounding him. He counted the limos he could see for something to do. He watched shoppers and tourists with cameras. He was used to sitting, used to watching, used to waiting. He had few expectations. But he was aware, this morning, of an underlying excitement—the off-hand chance that he might see Dorothy Lamont again.

Dino Giovanni arrived around eleven. Just like in his photo, he was immaculately manicured. His dark wavy hair was still full. There was a touch of gray in his temples. He wore expensive slacks, with a sleeveless safari jacket over a white shirt. His shoes were slender, likely Italian. And there was a youthful spring in his step, Gallow noted. Why not? The guy seemed to have it all.

The day was uneventful, Giovanni going about his business with the others. He stayed mostly on the phone with his feet propped on the Lucite desk. He kept his gaze turned out the window most the time as he talked. Gallow decided he wasn't so much looking out as he was posing for those looking in.

As the day dragged on, a couple of clients came and went—nobody famous that Gallow recognized. At one point he had to move his car to let a delivery truck have access to the space. He took the opportunity to make a run by the Seven-Eleven, use the restroom, and pick-up a burger from Wendy's. He was back in his spot in less than an hour, picking up where he'd left off. Nothing changed.

Throughout the day, Gallow would think of Dorothy Lamont. The image of her would pop into his head—the nubile daughter of the Russian Czar, and he would try to put it away.

Around seven that evening Giovanni left, and Gallow followed him home—the home of Dorothy Lamont. The house was located off Laurel Canyon, and was set behind a security gate. It was one of those cantilevered jobs, all glass, which seemed to defy gravity at the edge of the cliff. The only conceivable entrance was through the gate. He pictured Dorothy inside, lounged on a sofa, a panoramic view of Hollywood beyond the glass. In the picture, she wore a silky bathrobe, tied at the waist; her feet were tucked beneath her; there was a fashion magazine across her lap, a glass of champagne in her flawless hand. Gallow sat watching the house, thinking of Dorothy. It was late into the night before he left.

Gallow made it through Tuesday trying to stay focused on the job, and not on his employer; Wednesday was much the same. He followed Dino and Jonathan to a deli down the street, where they had lunch, before returning to the studio. On Friday, Dino stopped at the Beverly Wilshire Hotel after work and had a drink, alone, at the bar before going home.

Over the weeks to come, Gallow met with Dorothy on several occasions to report that nothing suspicious with Dino had occurred. They met in private, in dark corners of parking garages or quiet overlooks along Mulholland Drive. Dorothy, as always, was incognito; Gallow always in awe.

Their visits were brief. But in those times, Gallow would discover more and more about Dorothy Lamont, all of which he loved. He confirmed her beauty with tiny glimpses behind the glasses, learned she had a sense of humor. And discovered, despite the gravesite get-up she always wore, she could be warm. She confided in him, at times, leaving casual touches on his arm, telling Gallow how she hated being alone. Telling him how secluded her big house could become, nights her husband didn't come home. How the Hollywood Hills could be a fearful place when you were a woman all alone.

Gallow could feel the pull. He considered offering to come stay with her. But knew he could not.

Instead, he offered his gun, a back-up from the glove compartment. "Just for protection," he told her, leaning close enough to smell her soft perfume, as he showed her how to set the safety. "I couldn't live with myself if anything happened to you."

Over the next few weeks, Gallow continued to surveil Dino Giovanni, while fantasizing about the man's wife. He would lie in bed and ponder the cruelty of gods who would place him in contact with such a beauty without ever allowing him to have her. He would dream of the two of them together, touching hands across a candle lit table; the two of them, naked, side by side on sheets that smelled of perfume...he couldn't help it. And he couldn't help one other thing, Gallow realized...he couldn't help falling in love.

Friday arrived, Giovanni lunched with Jonathan again. Gallow was beginning to think Dorothy Lamont had gotten it all wrong. Her husband, Giovanni, was more of a Boy Scout than a philanderer. Gallow had not seen even one thing to suggest the man had something going on the side. That evening, Giovanni stepped to the sidewalk outside the studio, where he was met by his wife, none other than Dorothy Lamont. Gallow felt a pang of resentment.

He followed them to a restaurant at the Marina, where a valet parked the car. Dorothy, as always, was incognito behind dark glasses and dressed in a simple unpretentious pantsuit. A scarf again covered her head, but there was no mistaking the poise, the practiced dignity he'd come to know.

The two ate quietly on the patio, saying little, but occasionally gazing off toward the sunset. At eight-thirty, Dorothy dropped Giovanni where she'd found him, on the sidewalk in front of the studio. He would work into the night, Gallow believed, and fall asleep on the sofa behind the window. She would go home. And there she would be, alone.

Gallow wanted desperately to follow her. He could meet her at the gated entrance and offer to come inside. They could share a drink, maybe, and he could get to know her outside the working environment.

Gallow did follow. He watched her drive inside. Watched the gated entrance close behind her. And when sunrise came, Gallow retired to his home.

Lying in bed, he made the decision that it was time to end his infatuation with Dorothy Lamont. And that meant ending his employment with her as well. His services were apparently a waste, and his growing obsession was doing him no good. He would give her a final report later in the day and tell her that, to the best of his knowledge, her husband was being faithful. It killed him to think he wouldn't see her again, but he resolved that it was for the best.

Drifting into sleep, he said, "John Gallow, old buddy…Dorothy Lamont is becoming dangerous to your health."

Gallow awoke Saturday afternoon to pounding.

"John Gallow?" a little man at the door said.

He was potbellied, in his fifties, with a narrow mustache that didn't quite reach the corners of his mouth. He had one of those Chicago accents, Gallow thought—a sort of Polish-sausage-up-the-nose condition that annoyed him. "I'm Detective Percy Kazinski. I'm wit' the Los Angeles Police Department. Homicide," he said. "This is my partner, Lester Davis."

"I know Lester," Gallow said. The two had shared drinks at a cop bar on Grand. He'd had dinner at his house a couple of times. He added, "How you doing, Les?"

"Good, John," Lester said.

"We'd like to ask you some questions, you don't mind," Kazinski said.

Gallow stepped back and let Kazinski and Davis inside, and followed them through a small foyer, to the living room, where he gestured them to the sofa. Gallow took a seat across from them.

Kazinski said nothing at first but seemed to study the décor. The room was sparsely decorated: a sofa, a recliner, a small drink stand next to it. The dining room across the way was empty. There were newspapers and magazines scattered on the floor. Gallow offered, "I divorced two years ago. I got the house, the wife got everything in it."

"So that would make you a single man," Kazinski said. It was more of a statement than a question.

"I suppose so," Gallow said.

"Mister Gallow, do you know a Missus Dorothy Li'mont?"

Gallow considered a reason for the question. He said hesitantly, "Yes, she's a client of mine."

"Client?" Kazinski said.

"She hired me to do a job."

"Well, I'd say your employment has been officially terminated, Mister Gallow."

Gallow shook his head. "I don't understand."

"She's dead, John," Lester Davis offered. "Dorothy Lamont is dead."

The news hit Gallow hard. He knew the investigative drill; Kazinski would be watching him closely to gauge his reaction. Gallow stared at the sober faces across from him; his own face, he imagined, twisted in confusion.

Kazinski said, "You sure you didn't already know that?"

"Know? No, you're just now telling me, aren't you?" Gallow took a moment. "How?" he finally asked.

"Shot once through the back of the head as she slept."

Jesus! Gallow thought. He put his face in his hands.

Kazinski said, "What we know, Mister Gallow, is that a surveillance camera at the front gate shows Missus Lamont arriving at her home apprax'imately forty minutes after dropping her husband at his studio. Ten minutes later, according to the recorded surveillance, you arrive in front of the house."

"So what? I told you she was a client. She hired me to watch her husband. I kept an eye on the place and went home sometime early this morning."

"The husband says he spent the night at his studio."

"Yes, I suppose he did. I never saw him come home."

"So you could attest that no one, not Mister Giovanni nor anyone else, came or went from the house the entire night."

"That's right. You've got the surveillance recording, check it, you'll see."

Kazinski and Davis shared a look. Kazinski said, "That's where there seems to be a prab'lem."

"A problem?"

"John," Lester Davis said, "the camera goes blank around ten minutes after your arrival. We place the estimated time of Lamont's death at approximately midnight. You say you were there the entire night...?" He shrugged. "It doesn't look good."

Gallow was starting to get it now; he was a suspect. He said, "So, you think I did it? Why would I? What's my motive."

"We have other recordings, other nights, Mister Gallow. You ever hear of stalking? You seem to spend an inordinate amount of time watching Missus Li'mont, when you claim to be watching the husband." Kazinski rose, and turned toward the foyer. "I'm not charging you at this time, you understand. But I wouldn't go anywhere if I were you."

Lester Davis came to his feet. "Don't worry, John. Something will come up." He joined Kazinski at the front door and the two left.

Gallow tried putting aside images of Dorothy Lamont with her head blown off. How was it possible? Giovanni couldn't have done it, nor anyone else. He was right there outside the gate. And that house—Jesus!—perched on a cliff like that, there was no other way in or out. How? Who?

Gallow didn't have answers. He was remembering those nights—crazy obsession—when he would sit outside Dorothy's house and try to picture her: Dorothy moving about her chambers; Dorothy mixing a drink; Dorothy bathing; Dorothy sliding her delicate body beneath the covers; Dorothy in the throws of passion, passion he fantasized he was delivering. It was true, there was no professional reason to be hanging around outside her house. Especially when Giovanni wasn't home. It was boyish longing—something he could neither rationalize nor explain to Detective Kazinski.

So how, then, did Dorothy end up murdered? No one wanted an answer to that question more than Gallow. He drove to the crime scene—the cantilevered house in the Hollywood Hills. There was a sentry posted at the gated entrance. Investigators were still at work inside and around the grounds, and there were news vans crowding the street in front.

Sitting there, at a distance from the house, Gallow pictured Dorothy as he had seen her many times over the past four weeks, a cloistered version of the starlet that also appeared on-screen before his eyes—this one silky, sexy, sensuous, with fire lighting her eyes. These images were followed by dark tableaus: Dorothy sprawled naked, lifeless, facedown across the bed, drowning in a pool of her own blood, her blonde hair soaking in it. Oh, Christ!

Gallow drove to a bar where he drank to intoxication. *Dino Giovanni*, he thought, chasing whiskey with beer...Why was Dorothy Lamont so convinced he was seeing another woman?

Gallow left the bar, feeling fogged in. He stopped at a liquor store and bought a pint of Jim Beam, not wanting the haze to fade. Outside Giovanni's studio, he drank from the pint and watched the windows above. It was dark inside and he could see no movement. He was just about to leave when Giovanni appeared from the street-level entrance. Jonathan was with him and the two made their way, chatting casually, to Giovanni's Mercedes parked at the curb. Gallow followed them to a restaurant up the coast near Malibu. He took a seat at the bar and sipped Brandy Alexanders as Giovanni and his swishy little dressmaker ate dinner.

They seemed at ease with each other—Giovanni seemed all too at ease period, considering he'd just lost his wife. They ate, talked, and laughed occasionally, as business partners might.

And they touched.

Gallow noticed. Could it be? "Dino has this little faggot named Jonathan who actually creates the designs," Gallow remembered Dorothy saying.

Gallow drained the rest of his drink and got out of there. He didn't like the way he felt; he didn't like the direction his mind was running. His cell phone was ringing as he slid behind the wheel. The day was ugly and about to turn uglier.

"They found the murder weapon, John," Lester Davis said on the other end of the phone. "A dumpster at the end of the street. The gun is registered to you."

The gun, Gallow thought. He'd forgotten all about it.

"You think I killed her?" Gallow asked.

"I'm giving you a heads-up, John, I owe you that. Their pursuing an arrest warrant now."

Gallow ended the call tossing his cell phone on the seat next to him. He headed north on Pacific Coast Highway.

At an overlook up the coast, Gallow sat and watched the waves, and sobered. It was funny really how quick you could fall for someone. Had he really been in love?

When the haze finally cleared and all that he was left with was a headache, Gallow drove back down the coast toward Malibu. He stopped at the Malibu Inn for something to eat. It was casual chic, with celebrity photos lining the walls, hundreds of them. He ordered the open-face turkey sandwich and drank black coffee as he scanned the headshots: Kirk Douglas, James Dean, Marilyn Monroe…He wondered if Dorothy Lamont's photo was somewhere in the mix. Barbara Streisand, Michael Douglas, Broderick Crawford…

Gallow finished his meal slowly and paid his bill. He was just about to push through the door and into the night, when an incomparable and unmistakable photo caught his eye. There, beyond the end of the bar—Dorothy Lamont.

Gallow crossed through the bar to the wall where her photo hung. He gazed up upon her, in reverence, as a man might in witnessing *The Pieta* for the first time. She seemed expectant in this photo, looking off to some other place and time. It was her, alright, Dorothy Lamont, but…

There was something wrong about it, Gallow thought.

Her face, her eyes, her proud aura…yet…It was the signature that was troubling him, he realized, the autograph.

Gallow left the bar and returned to his car. On the back seat lay the manila envelope Dorothy Lamont had given him. Inside was the list of contacts and places, and the photo of Giovanni, but on the outside of the envelope was the autograph he'd sheepishly asked her for that first night in the restaurant. Gallow took the envelope back into the bar and compared it to the signed photo on the wall. They were different—Christ!—decidedly different.

Thoughts were rushing at him. If the signature on the envelope wasn't Dorothy Lamont's then the woman he'd met in the bar was not Dorothy Lamont…and if that woman was not Dorothy, then who…?

"I saw her once in person." The comment came from a guy at the bar. He was watching Gallow, saying, "She used to come in here."

"Here?" Gallow said. "You recognized her?"

"No mistaking that beauty," the man at the bar said. "Nice lady, too. She'd sign autographs, chat up the waiters. Very outgoing person for a celebrity."

Gallow felt sick to his stomach. It was obvious. The woman who had hired him—worse!—the woman he'd fallen desperately in love with, was not Dorothy Lamont.

But who?

Gallow wasn't sure, but there was a thought nagging at him. He left quickly and drove back down the coast, remembering—shit, picturing!—the long fingers, the delicate slender hands that had reached to him, had touched him gently on several occasions. From the folder, Gallow acquired an address and drove to an apartment in West Hollywood.

He made his way through a garden setting, to a landing above the pool. Below, the aquamarine water shimmered in the surrounding darkness, jazz music filtered from one of the other units. He let himself in with a lock-pick and went to work.

Breaking and entering? No. Investigating was what he was doing, something he realized he'd been neglecting to do these past weeks—his head up his ass in boyish love. Moving through the apartment with the small penlight he'd taken from his glove compartment, he tossed drawers, and rummaged closets. He wasn't sure what he was looking for, but he was damn sure convinced he would know it when he saw it.

Nothing in the bedroom or in the kitchen or in the bath. Then, from a bookshelf in the main living area, Gallow removed a scrapbook. It was filled with photos, playbills, newspaper clippings, and other memorabilia. The pieces fell into place. Remembering the feelings he'd had these last four weeks, the tender and sometimes erotic dreams that had played in his head nightly, he wanted to vomit.

What an elaborate set-up, Gallow thought.

And what a dolt he'd been to fall for it.

Before Gallow could completely come to terms with his realizations, the door burst open and lights came on.

"Don't move!" he heard, and blinked to adjust his sight.

Two Uniformed Policemen were standing, academy stance, guns drawn. Detective Kazinski waddled casually into the apartment. Followed by Lester Davis.

"I expected you to be on a bus for the border by now, Mister Gallow," Kazinski said. "But our uniforms ran your plate double-parked in the alley."

Gallow was still standing before the bookshelf, the scrapbook open in his hands, he said, "I know who killed Dorothy Lamont."

"Can we expect a confession?" Kazinski said.

"The person who killed Dorothy Lamont was the one having the affair with Dino Giovanni. The same person I've been foolishly tripping over my tongue for these past few weeks. And the same person you saw on the surveillance camera, that you mistakenly thought was Dorothy Lamont arriving at the residence. Fact is…" Gallow said, "I've never actually met the movie star, Dorothy Lamont, as it turns out. And the night she was killed, she never even left the house. I suppose you didn't back the tape up far enough to discover that. She was home all along."

"Then who went to dinner with Giovanni, who dropped him at the curb, and who, if I might ask, is on the tape arriving at the Lamont home, just after said dinner?"

Gallow handed the opened scrapbook to Kazinski and watched as he read from a playbill. He read slowly, pronouncing each phrase aloud with intentional deliberation. "Jonathan Ferryman…appearing nightly at the 'Kit Kat

Kaberet'...three blocks from the Vegas Strip...Celebrity Female Impersonator Extraordinaire."

Kazinski began slowly flipping pages, studying the photos inside. "There's Cher," he said. "A Carol Channing." Another page, he said, "We got a Lucille Ball, and a Barbara Streisand..."

"And there's one very important one," Gallow added.

He watched until Kazinski turned the page, then headed for the door. He heard behind him, "...and, interestingly, we got a Dorothy Lamont."

Gallow slipped into the night and made his way toward the street. At the car, he turned the key in the door, then paused and dropped his head. The slogan, "It's better to have loved and lost..." entered his mind. No, that didn't quite fit. He opened the door and slid behind the wheel. Starting the engine, he said, "It's better to have never met your love, than..."

No that didn't work either. Okay, so he'd work on it.

Gallow pulled away from the curb. He'd go home, have a stiff drink, a couple of them. But first he'd stop at a video store, rent a movie: the one about the budding daughter of the Russian Czar, who gets ravaged by Rasputin, Rumplestiltskin, whatever the hairy guy's name was...and then, just maybe then, somewhere in the night, he'd fall in love with a movie star all over again. This time, the way it was meant to happen for a lowly PI like him...*Only in the movies.*

A RESPECTABLE
PERIOD OF
MOURNING

Honoria Fintescu hoped she wasn't being inappropriate, inviting her friend, Eleanor Plum, for tea, so soon after her husband's death. There was, after all, a respectable period of mourning expected before one began to accept visitors.

The closeness of the community—Sun Vista Retirement Village, where they lived—would have allowed Eleanor to walk the short distance to Honoria's bungalow, but with Eleanor's arthritis, Honoria insisted that Naldo, one of the Salvadoran gardeners, drive her in his cart.

"He's cleaning the Koi pond today," Honoria told her over the phone. "But he's such a sweet boy. He'll do just about anything I ask. Shall we say ten o'clock?"

Honoria prepared a tea service and placed it on the screened-in porch, hoping to catch the morning breeze. At precisely ten, Eleanor arrived; a shirtless and brown-skinned Naldo waited in his cart at the curb until she had carefully navigated the path to the entrance. Honoria was at the door to greet her.

"Eleanor, dear, thanks so much for coming. I so needed someone to talk to." Her voice was that of a lark

They hugged, Eleanor stepping away to say, "Honoria, let me take a look at you. You look marvelous under the circumstances. The scarf makes you look so Bette Davis."

"The young Bette or the old Bette?" Honoria inquired.

"We'll let's not kid ourselves, dear," Eleanor said. "But really, how are you holding up?"

"Better…better…" Honoria said, "it was a shock at first, you know. But better now." Now she took time to wave Naldo goodbye. "Thank you, Naldo, dear."

"De nada, Missus F. I'll see you at nightfall, chica?"

"He calls me 'Chica,'" Honoria said, placing a hand on Eleanor's forearm. "Isn't that sweet?"

They ducked inside for morning tea.

They were in their early eighties, Honoria and Eleanor. Both were frail little vessels, grandmothers and great-grandmothers to youngsters scattered back east. Honoria's hair was thick and cottony white, while Eleanor's had grown thin and had turned a rusted orange. Both had spindly little legs, but where Honoria's could go all day, Eleanor's required her to take careful, measured steps. Both had found their husbands in their early twenties, and had been married countless years. Now Honoria's husband was gone.

They sat in silence for a time on the screened-in porch, sipping tea from delicately patterned China and looking out onto the fairways and greens of the Sun Vista Retirement Village Golf Course. A light desert breeze teased the oleanders and cactus flowers that defined the small backyard. Sparrows played in and out of sprawling Bougainvillea. The morning brought a sweet delicate peace to the patio.

After a time, Eleanor said, "I want to say I'm so sorry for your loss, dear. It must be terribly difficult losing a husband."

"You would think so," Honoria said. "I thought the place would feel empty with Newell passing on. But it just feels roomier, if you can understand the difference."

"Me, I worry the quiet will get to me once Howard is gone."

Honoria gave it some thought. "Yes, I considered that, I suppose. There was always the drone of CNN and Sports Center throughout the house. But, I have to say, I'm beginning to adjust to the peace and quiet. And, of course, the freedom. Except for the walk Newell took in the foothills each morning, he was always underfoot. I never had what you would actually call a minute's peace."

"Why is it" Eleanor said, "men spend all their younger years looking for outlets to escape spending time with their wives—work, business trips, golf, drinking buddies—and the minute they retire, they're on us like lint on wool? My husband, Howard, never leaves the house. Doesn't do a thing. I don't dare invite company. He sits and listens to every word. Like a child. Can you imagine?"

"I know. 'Twenty-four-seven!'" Honoria said. "That's something Naldo would say."

Unable to keep a mischievous twinkle from her eye, Eleanor said, "You seem very close to Naldo, dear."

Honoria looked at her flatly. "It's because he's so good in bed."

She managed a straight face just long enough to carry the moment, then both women burst out laughing.

They laughed until they cried.

When the revelry finally subsided, Honoria said, "No, Naldo's just a sweet boy who helps all the windowed ladies of Sun Vista Village. He calls us 'Babes' and 'Chicas'...calls Cynthiana Lowery 'Miss February'...if can you imagine. She's eighty-six years old. No, just a sweet boy. You haven't been here that long. But you'll see."

"I think I'm beginning to," Eleanor said and turned her gaze to the vista beyond the porch.

The women sat sipping their tea in silence for a time; as a family of Gamble's Quail—mamma and a string of babies, their top notches bobbing to a beat—paraded their way from the fairway and off into the foliage.

After a time, Honoria, her tone more serious now, said, "I hope I didn't appear disrespectful, dear, calling so soon after Newell's death." She sipped daintily from her cup, her pinky upturned. "But I was anxious to find closure, as they say. Bring a new sense of order to my life you understand."

Sipping, then sitting her cup aside and folding her hands in front of her, Eleanor said, "Personally, I never understood this whole concept of having a respectable period of mourning. I mean, really, how long is long enough? But there is one thing I question..." She paused. "What do you do with the body?"

Together, the two women turned their gaze inside, beyond the door leading onto the porch. There on the kitchen floor, no more than ten feet away, lay Honoria's husband, Newell. He was face down on the tile, still in his morning boxers and undershirt. An ugly indentation showed at the back of his scalp. His thinning hair was caked and matted with blood. Next to him, on the floor, a heavy iron skillet lay abandoned. It too was smudged with dried, cakey gore.

"Well," Honoria said, studying her husband's body from across the porch, "he'll be taken far up the hiking trail he usually takes and dropped off a hillside. The coroner will rule it an accident. 'Poor old senile soul wandered off the path.'"

Eleanor nodded. She studied the body that lay on the kitchen tile, then carefully stood and made her way over to survey it more closely. "What about the others?" she said. "Did they all fall off the trail?"

From her place at the table, Honoria said, "Of course not, dear. They all have their 'thing.' Lucy Draco's husband was found face up in the pool. He swims, you know. Cynthiana's husband just fell down the steps. My God, the man was ninety-seven. Who would question?"

Eleanor studied the body for a moment longer, then returned to her seat on the porch. She took up her tea and sipped at it. After a thoughtful moment, she said, "And what do you think we should do with my husband, Howard? I mean, how can I be sure it will look natural…Howard doesn't have a 'thing.'"

Honoria patted Eleanor's hand reassuringly. "Don't worry, dear. Naldo will take care of it. Did I mention what a sweet boy he is?"

THE FREE AGENT

Wakefulness came slowly. Like being at the bottom of a dark lake and having to wait while you float to the surface for light.

His instincts told him he had something to remember. But what? He was Eddie Robison, that much he knew: star centerfielder for the Cincinnati Reds; had been Rookie of the Year his first year there. And he was turning free agent this next season. Was that it? Was that what he needed to remember? No.

He remembered flying to Atlanta. Yes, and had arrived there. Met with Brave's Management about a deal to start in centerfield next season. Was it six million for twelve years, or twelve million for six years? He wasn't sure. But he remembered, now, having lunch with Ted Turner—Mister Turner—and having asked something about what they planned to do with Jimmy Kendricks, the veteran that currently occupied the position. Turner saying: "Hell boy, we'll put floppy ears on Kendricks and use him for a mascot if that's what it takes to get you signed." He remembered calling him Ted after that.

There was still something nagging at the edge of recollection, something important he thought. And…why was it so damned hard to open his eyes?

It came to him slowly…the ride around town after the meetings. Peachtree Street. The Underground. Then out into the countryside. Tall Georgia pines. Sweet smells. Stone Mountain. Confederate Generals charging into battle across a granite face. The drive back toward the city along Buford Highway and, wait…

Headlights veered across the double-yellow line. There was blinding light, the agonizing screech of tires. And that sickening noise: the sound of glass and metal fighting violently for the same space. That's what was pulling at him, dragging him toward wakefulness. He had been in an accident. A terrible, terrible accident.

Eddie opened his eyes to see a phosphor-green trace skipping across the black screen of a heart monitor. Heard its bleep-bleep-bleep. He was in a hospital. He was lying in bed. A single nightlight cast dull shadows about the room. There was a gagging mixture of bleach and illness in the air. His surroundings dull white.

To Eddie's right was a partially drawn curtain. The lower half of an adjoining bed could be seen extending beyond it. He was aware of silence. He was aware of dull pain inside his head, and stiffness in his left arm. And he was aware of one more thing—a complete and total void of sensation below the covers.

"Somebodeee!"

There was no response, then…

"You have to push the button if you want them to come."

The voice came from the adjoining bed, surprising him. A man's voice.

"What?"

"The button, the one on the end of the cord. You gotta press it, you want Nurse Ritter to come."

"What's wrong with me? I can't feel my legs."

A silence hung in the air. Eddie strained to try to see past the curtain, all he could make out was the man's lower half: a mounded midsection and thick legs beneath the hospital sheets.

"I'm sorry," the man said. "It's probably not for me to say, but you do seem upset."

"What! What do you know?"

"Well…" The man coughed heavily, a ragged smokers hack, and there was another moment of silence in which Eddie wondered if the man had stopped breathing. Finally the man continued. "I did hear Nurse Ritter talking to the doc. They said something about a spinal injury. 'Bout how you may never walk again."

A mewling, whimpering sound began at the knot that had formed in Eddie's throat. He choked it back, the effort causing it to come out in little blasts of mucus through his nose. He could taste it, salty, where it ran to his lips. Tears pooled in his eyes.

No! he thought. This can't happen! "I need to see the nurse!" he said.

Eddie searched the bedding, came up with the call-button. He pressed it— pressed it again—then tossed it angrily aside to wait.

"I'm sorry I told you," the man behind the curtain said. "That wasn't right of me. I'm sure they'll get you into some kind of physical therapy, maybe, get you into one of those walkers or something…"

"Just shut up, will you!" Eddie said. "I'm going to talk to them and get to the bottom of this thing."

The nurse arrived on a cloud of lilac scented perfume. Sonny Ritter: young and blonde and voluptuous, spilling in critical places from her clean, white nurses uniform.

She didn't look like any caregiver Eddie had ever seen. She was one of those women who could stir a man, any man, with just a look, get anything she wanted. The idea struck Eddie, making him painfully aware there were no stirrings beneath *his* sheets. Just deadness from the waist down. He choked back another sob.

She ignored him, at first, going straight for the clipboard that dangled at the foot of his bed. Then, consulting a small gold watch, she made a notation.

When she finally looked up, it was not at him, but across the room to the man on the other bed.

"How're we doing, Mr. Simms?" Her voice was deep and as sultry as Eddie imagined it might be. "Feeling a little stronger tonight?"

"Like I could bench press a Volvo," Simms replied, sarcastically.

"I saw your son came by to visit earlier. Didn't that make you feel a little better?"

"Yeah. Oh, hey! Did I tell you he's going out for track next year?"

The small talk was infuriating.

"That's great, Wesley. Tell him I know he'll be a star."

"God damn it, Nurse!" Eddie's patience had run out.

Nurse Ritter's gaze came slowly around to meet his. Despite his agitation, his fear and worry, Eddie calmed. The pools of her eyes were so blue and so deep, he considered, a man standing too close to them might just tumble in and never be heard from again. Suggestiveness played at her lips, and when she finally spoke, the voice was low and seductive.

"You can call me Sonny, Mr. Robinson. What can I do for you?"

"There's something I have to know," Eddie said. He nodded toward the other bed. "Is it true what he told me? Am I paralyzed?"

Nurse Ritter turned a disapproving look on Simms. "Talking out of school again, Wesley?" Then to Eddie. "I'm sorry. The injury is to the spinal cord."

"But…what?…there must be something you can do? There's pills…surgery…there's…nerve implants…they must have nerve implants! Something!"

"There's nothing we can do. I'm sorry."

"Don't you know who I am? I'm Eddie Robinson! I hit over three hundred last season…thirty-six home runs…I stole twenty-nine bases!"

Sonny Ritter held Eddie's eyes solemnly for several seconds, then said, "I know who you are, Eddie. And I'm impressed. But apparently the drunk that hit you wasn't a baseball fan. I'm sorry." She approached the bed and leaned in to fish for the lost call-button. Her uniform parted at the bodice and gave him a glimpse of untold riches.

"If there's anything I can get for you," she said, her face just inches from his, "just call."

And with that she placed the button in his hand and departed, leaving only a lilac scented memory behind.

"She sure is something, ain't she?" Simms said, from the next bed. "I'd like to park my car in her garage, if you know what I mean?"

Eddie wasn't in the mood for it. He had things to consider. Options to work out. Contingencies to plan.

"So you're Eddie Robinson, the ballplayer?" Simms continued. "Man, that's a damned shame. My kid, Greg, is a fan of yours, talks about you all the time. And to think I'm lying here in bed, right across from you."

"Yeah, to think," Eddie said, wishing the man would just shut the hell up.

"You know…as strange as it may seem, we have a lot in common." Simms coughed once then wheezed.

"Yeah…?" Eddie said.

Try as he might, he could not imagine what Eddie Robinson, two time Golden Glove winner and possibly the number one babe-magnet in the National League, could possibly have in common with this tuberculin burn-out.

"What's that?" he asked anyway, not caring about the answer.

"Well, you and me," Simms said, "we both kind of had our dreams, and now…." he became solemn, "and now, well…your dream is gone, gotta be, right at its peak. And mine? I needed five more good years…selling years that is…and I could have gotten my kid through college. I never got the chance for a real education, myself. I sell insurance, you see. It's a tough job. Always humpin' to make quota. Talkin' about financial security and the unfair risks life offers. Never quite making enough to pay the bills."

Eddie listened, despite himself, preferring to get back to his thoughts.

"I just didn't want Greg to end up like me. Damn, I love that boy. He's the whole world to me." Simms sighed heavily and wheezed. "But, now, they tell me

I'll never work again. Guess he'll wind up just like his old man. Burned-up, stressed-out, heart pumping air by the age of forty-eight. Man, it's a cruel world."

"Don't you have disability insurance?" Eddie asked, the solution seeming obvious.

"Well now, therein lies the problem. You see, I've a got a one-hundred-thousand-dollar term life policy from the company, but…" he paused, "I never took out any disability. Ironic don't you think? Dead, I'm worth a college degree and then some. Alive, I ain't worth bubble-gum to a flat tire. I guess it does seem pretty stupid, me being an insurance salesman and all. But it's typical. It's always the plumber with the leaky faucets. And it's the doctor that smokes a half-pack of cigarettes a day. Guess we're good at fixin' everybody but ourselves."

"Yeah, well, I'm real torn up about Greg's education, but I've got some problems of my own right now."

"I understand," Simms said. "Anyway, I do have a plan."

"Really? And what's that?" Eddie asked.

The man on bed extended his hand beyond the curtain and proffered a small instrument. "This," he said.

Eddie craned his neck to see through the jumble of tubes and cables. "Looks like a syringe."

"It is a syringe," Simms said, proudly. "I swiped it off the tray when they were working on you."

"How does that help?" Eddie asked. He was mildly curious.

"You know what happens when you pump an empty syringe full of air into an artery."

Eddie thought about it. "I understand it creates a bubble that when it reaches the heart can kill you."

"Bingo," Simms said. "All I have to do is thump-up a plump vein, insert the pointy end of this little baby, then pump off a wad of stale air, and pop! goes the heart. And the best part is, no one will ever know. Cardiac arrest, natural causes. The insurance company pays off, and little Greg collects and goes to college."

"Except you'll be dead," Eddie said, doubting Simms's sincerity. "Doesn't that bother you?"

"Well, some, I have to admit. You've had a good run in your short years, but me…All I ever wanted was to help my son have a better life than the one I've had. And, now, he will, after I'm gone." Simms's voice became conspiratorial. "I was figuring on doing it tonight."

Eddie tried to picture what the man behind the curtain might look like. What he imagined was a huge round face, bloated with sagging jowls, cheeks fiery from the flush of high blood pressure. Maybe veins exploding in patterns across his nose.

"Does this damned curtain have to stay pulled?" Eddie said.

"No rules, I guess," Simms replied. "Maybe we can get Nurse Bombshell to pull it back next time so we can talk proper."

"What I don't get," Eddie said, "is you don't sound overly afraid of dying."

"Dying? Dying's the easy part. Though I would have liked to been around to see Greg graduate. No, dying's not bad like most people think, it's actually beautiful."

"Beautiful?" Eddie said, skeptical.

"That's right. More beautiful than anything you've ever imagined. And trust me, I've had some experience with dying. The day they brought me in my heart had been stopped for more than four minutes. And the things I saw during that time, the things I learned...Actually, I shouldn't be saying anything."

"Why's that?" Eddie asked.

"Because it all sounds too crazy. People might start thinking I suffered brain damage during those four minutes."

Simms hesitated, then said, "Well, what the heck. I've needed to tell someone about it for some time now. But you've got to promise me you'll trust that I'm telling you the truth, the absolute truth, as I've experienced it. Promise?"

"Yeah, sure, whatever," Eddie said.

"All right. It was during my heart attack, the day they brought me in. There I was in the emergency room, on the bed. Doctors were pounding on me; nurses were pumpin' air into my chest like I was a rubber doll they were anxious to inflate. I was out. Stone cold dead they tell me. But I was watching all this, every second of it. Not from the table like you might expect. Jesus, Mary and Joseph, no! I was somewhere up above, along the ceiling it was, looking down at myself laying on the table. I was down here, but I was up there all at the same time. You see what I'm saying?"

"A near death experience," Eddie said. "I've heard of them, but I never put much stock in them."

"Well, let me tell you, you can put stock in them, baby brother. Blue Chip stock, 'cause it happened to me. I could see and hear everything that was being done to my body, but I wasn't inside it at the time. No, sir! Then, just like they tell you, I just sort of rotated in mid-air, faced upward, and passed right through the ceiling. I actually had the instinct to duck as I went through, believe it or not. I just slid through the roof, like a cold draft, and directly into a dark tunnel. I was floating at first, then I picked up speed. It reminded me of that...what do you call it?...hyperspace, I think it is. Anyway...

Eddie suspended his disbelief momentarily and fell into the rhythm of Simms's story. He wondered about the bright light you hear of. Come toward the light, they say. And then Simms was telling him about it.

"...I could see a dot of light in the distance. And as I sped along, it got bigger and bigger, until it was the size of a tent flap. And bright. I knew...though I don't know how...that I was supposed to step into that light; step *through* the light. So, I did."

Eddie could hear Simms's breathing. It was labored. He felt for the man with the bad heart whose experience had affected him so. Then he heard Simms's breathing suddenly smooth. When he spoke again, his voice had become clear and peaceful.

"It was the most wonderful thing I'd ever seen. They welcomed me in and I was overcome with love, I tell you. It was a world without resistance. I had freedom of movement that I hadn't felt in years, maybe ever. Every thought in my head was crystal clear, as if all the questions of life and the universe were suddenly answered."

Simms became suddenly quiet. After a moment he broke the silence.

"That's all I can tell you," he said. "I don't have words that will properly describe the rest. The next thing I knew, I snapped back. I was back on the table and inside my body again, and the pain was unbearable."

Eddie tried to come to terms with the idea. Tried searching his mind for other, more reasonable, explanations for what Simms believed he had experienced. He found none. Simms was convinced it was real and spoke with the conviction of a diehard Evangelist. Perhaps there were things beyond understanding, Eddie acknowledged to himself. Perhaps there is knowledge we are privileged to only in death. What was that saying in the Bible? Something about all things being revealed in heaven. Maybe he didn't know as much as he thought he did.

"...I heard the doctors congratulating themselves," Simms was saying, "and Nurse Ritter holdin' my hand. But I'll tell you, I was not celebrating with them. I hated them—then and for a time after—for bringing me back. So you ask about dying? Eddie...I can't wait!"

The man was clear in his conviction, that much was sure, Eddie realized. But was it worth dying for?

Eddie thought about his childhood. How at eight he would stand in the dusty fields of his father's farm and smack dirt clods with a hoe handle, watching them sail across the fence line. Even then, on that imaginary playing field, he would go three-for-four with a home run and two RBI's. At eleven he had hit a home run to win the Tri-State Little League Championship. He could still recall the sound the bat had made against the ball on that particular day. So sweet that sound remained, that home runs thereafter never sounded quite the same. In high school, he lead the team in stolen bases, took Championships both junior and senior years. Went straight to the minors, then up to the Bigs. With only games left in the American League East Division, he singled to drive in the winning run, clinching the pennant for the Reds. He had experience the exhilaration of the game, the roar of the crowds, and the love and admiration of fans. Baseball was his life. It was everything. And now…it would be over.

"Do they play baseball up there?" he asked.

He heard Simms grunt as if coming awake.

"What?"

"Up there…" Eddie said. "Heaven or whatever you want to call it. Do they play baseball?"

There was silence from behind the curtain. Simms giving it some thought, perhaps.

"Yeah," Simms finally said. "It can be whatever you want. That's why it's heaven."

"Would there be other teams, leagues? How about fans?" Eddie asked. "Would there be fans?"

"As many as the eye can see, if you want it that way," Simms replied. "But why are you asking, you're not gonna die?

"I've been thinking," Eddie said. "You dream of putting your son through college and being able to live long enough to see it. I dream of nothing but playing baseball, and I don't want to live without it."

"What are you saying, Eddie?"

"Mr. Simms…I'll pay you one-hundred-thousand dollars for your syringe, right now. It's the same amount as your Life Insurance Policy, only you'll be able to see your son graduate.

"Pay me? I don't know, Eddie. That doesn't sound so good."

"You were prepared to do it, weren't you? Were you telling me the truth about all that stuff?"

"Yes, that I'd swear by."

"Then that's it," Eddie said, gathering the call button. "I'll get Nurse Ritter to bring me my checkbook and it'll be done."

Nurse Ritter arrived instantly. "What can I do for you, Mister Robinson?"

"My personal effects, where are they?"

"They're right there," she said, pointing to the small closet near the doorway. "Is there something I can get for you?"

"My checkbook. Will you bring it to me please?"

Nurse Ritter crossed her arms beneath her breasts and looked Eddie over with a cool, surgical gaze.

"Your checkbook?" she said.

"In the breast pocket of my blazer, yes," Eddie said.

Sonny Ritter threw a sideways glance at Simms who lay quietly, without comment, behind the curtain. Then without further question she turned to the closet and retrieved the checkbook from Eddie's clothing.

"Will there be anything else?" she said, handing it across the bed to him.

"Just some privacy, please."

Sonny Ritter gave Eddie another wary look, then turned and left the room without comment.

Eddie quickly wrote the check, anxious to get it done before either one of them could back out. He removed the check, folded it once, and placed it atop the bedside tray. Then he placed the checkbook next to it. "There," he said. "You'll have to trust the check is good."

"I trust you, Eddie. Of course I do," Simms said. "Then toss me the syringe."

There was no immediate response from behind the curtain, and there was a moment where Eddie thought Simms might back out. Then, from behind curtain, the instrument lofted and tumbled end-for-end to land in Eddie's lap. Eddie felt nothing of the impact and resolved to follow through.

Neither man spoke. The room grew still. Only the rhythmic bleep of the heart monitor penetrated the silence. Then, with a suddenness that cried for attention, it burst into a long shrill tone. Then stopped.

Nurse Ritter entered the room unhurriedly and stood at the foot of Eddie's bed. Behind her, two orderlies appeared with a gurney. They loaded Eddie Robinson aboard, then disappeared with him, down the hall.

Sonny Ritter stood for a time with her arms crossed beneath her full breasts and stared at her white shoes.

"It's on the tray," Simms said.

Sonny lifted her eyes to the tray. She crossed to it and gathered the folded check. Unfolding it, she read aloud to Simms.

"Pay to the order of Mr. Wesley Simms, One-hundred-thousand-dollars. Signed, Edward L. Robinson."

Sonny Ritter turned to the curtain and drew it open. Wesley Simms was look-ing down his chin, to the hands folded atop his expansive midsection. Slowly, he raised his face to meet her.

The face was not fat. There no were jowls. There were no cracked or broken veins in the nose. The face looking back at Sonny was richly tanned and chiseled to a work of art. His wavy hair was black and stylishly coiffed. A broad smile slowly spread across his lips, revealing perfect rows of white teeth.

Sonny's smile drew characteristically seductive.

They held each other's gaze for several seconds, then burst into laughter.

Simms, better known as Johnny Devin to his friends and to Sonny Ritter, stripped back the sheet-covering and tossed aside the large pillow resting on his mid-section. Dressed in shorts and a tight, muscle-fitting t-shirt, he stepped from the bed and pulled Sonny into his embrace. They kissed long and hard. And when they broke at last for air, they gazed hotly into each other's eyes.

Sonny untangled herself from Johnny's arms and stepped to the center of the room, stopping deliberately, as if hitting her mark center-stage. She turned with a practiced poise, held the check out and kissed it grandly.

"You were sensational, darling," she said, "star, actor extraordinaire. And this one gig paid more than all the theater we've done, combined."

Johnny grinned a grin that made her, and virtually all women, weak in the knees.

"It was you, baby, brilliant," Devin replied. "Using a spinal tap to numb a ballplayer's legs. The one thing no athlete can live without."

"The greater the assets, the greater the loss," Sonny said.

"Was there anything really wrong with him?" he asked, now, sheepishly.

"Oh, a mild concussion," Sonny said, snapping the check, as if testing its elas-ticity. "He'd probably have had a whopping headache for a couple of days. That's about it."

She looked at Johnny and the two burst out laughing.

When their revelry had died down, he asked, "So, baby, what's next?"

"Well…I understand," Sonny said, giving Johnny a sly grin, "they picked up a fella out on Interstate Twenty who has run his car into a ditch, drunk, poor baby. They're bringing him in now. They say, he's a famous porn star," she said, giving Johnny another sly look and producing a large syringe of Novocain. "Think you can play this one…Mr. Simms?"

SWEATY MONEY

There was always the briefest moment of remorse before she killed a man, a half second of pity that threatened to chill her plan. But it was fleeting—there and gone. Experience told her it was no big deal.

Jana stood over Richie Cavo where he knelt in front of his safe. The combination had fallen into place, and the solid door was now hanging open. Feeling her at his shoulder, Richie looked up through drunken eyes, half surprised, half questioning, a stupid grin on his face. She placed the muzzle of the silenced .38 to the nape of his neck. "Bye-bye, Richie," she said, and squeezed off one round.

The bullet passed through the back of Richie's head and exited his left jaw, taking pieces of his partial plate and several real teeth with it. He dropped lifeless to a fetal position on the floor. There asshole! she told herself. What was there to feel sorry for?

The hit was a clean one. Something Jana hoped for on all her hits but never really expected. You could plan and plan...hell plan your ass off...and these things could still get FUBAR in a heartbeat.

FUBAR...she heard herself say.

It was lingo left over from her Marine Corp days, when her forward sniper unit would get caught behind enemy lines, inside Fallujah, and then things would get sideways in a hurry and—Christ!—all hell would break loose—machineguns, mortars, rockets, shit!—and the whole situation would get FUBAR. But that was then and this was now, Jana told herself. She was a civilian here in Richie's house, and the biggest enemy she faced was indecisiveness.

Jana checked outside. The night was quiet. The silencer had reduced the gun blast to nothing more than a popcorn fart, and the car in the driveway belonged to Richie. It was the stupid gumba's pride and joy, an older model, black Mercedes. It would be a fitting vehicle to carry him to his final resting place, some deep canyon waiting off Catalina Highway.

There was two-hundred-thousand-dollars in the safe. It took only minutes to gather it into a bag. She made her first trip to the car to stash it and her purse, with the gun inside, beneath the front seat. After, she returned to strip a rug from beneath the desk and roll Richie inside. That part was easy, but getting the linguini-slurping asshole into the car was going to be another matter.

Jana considered lifting one end of the rolled carpet, and getting under it, doing a crab crawl with it to the car, but, shit, then still have to lift the guy into the trunk.

What to do?

Trained to think on her feet, Jana returned to the car. She backed it quickly against the side porch railing and popped the trunk catch, leaving the lid ajar. She then went back inside to drag Richie and the rolled carpet onto the porch. It took kicking out a section of porch railing to accommodate the fat fucker, but with the section missing, she was able to roll him the last couple of feet, off and into the trunk. Jana slammed the lid. Done.

Back inside, Jana breathed a sigh of relief. All there was left to do was clean what was left of Richie off the linoleum, retrieve the .38 slug from the flooring, and eliminate any trace of fingerprints she might have left behind. The score had gone as planned. She had selected Richie out of dozens of possible marks as a guy who dealt in cash; taken weeks to get close to him, letting the fat guinea-asshole put his greasy hands all over; and she had meticulously planned how to kill him and take the money. It was scripted and rehearsed, down to the last detail. The one thing—the only thing—she could not have predicted or prepared for in a million-gazillion years...was the guy in the fucking tow truck.

Jana came out through the kitchen door, mop and pail in-hand, to see Richie's car disappearing off down the street, attached to a truck labeled *A-1 Towing*. Her purse—her driver's license, for Christ sake—was in the car with two-hundred-thousand-dollars in cash and a dead body. All that money in the safe and...what?...the stupid, gumba-fuck doesn't make his car payment?

Her last glimpse of her life as she knew it came as the tow truck made the corner, picked up speed, and disappeared.

*   *   *   *

Lougie dragged the black Mercedes south, down Craycroft and made a right on Broadway, Tucson traffic this time of night sparse, the locals and retired snowbirds secure behind deadbolt locks. There was a K-Mart two miles farther up, a large empty lot in which to drop the car. Crossing the intersection at Wilmot, navigating the tow rig and car easily along the inside lane, Lougie used his cell phone to call his buddy, Fremont, long distance in California.

"Man, you should be here," he said, hearing Fremont's voice come on. "I got this new way of scammin' some dough, dude."

Here was Lougie, in his worn jeans and Smashing Pumpkins t-shirt, talking money and scams to a guy who had just scored two-point-seven million off some dead guy, and was now wearing silk smoking jackets and living in a rented beach house in Malibu. He hoped Fremont could, at the least, appreciate the genius in his latest idea.

"Man, tell me what the fuck I want to be there for, the desert," Fremont said. "I got the ocean...the *Pacific*-fucking Ocean, understand...right out the back door. Girls in the teeny-weeniest of little bikinis drop by off the beach to toke my weed and anything else I ask."

Away from the phone, Lougie heard Fremont say, "Girl, pass me my drink, will you, sugar," then into the phone again say, "You dig what I'm saying? I keep telling you, my man, California is the land of opportunity. Haven't I been saying that? *You* should be *here*."

Every time Lougie spoke to Fremont, Fremont would have to tell him about *his* thing out there. How he was living the life, man. How ladies *was* hanging like oranges from the trees. Then he'd have to listen to him try to convince him to come out, join him.

California...shit!

Lougie couldn't see it: freeways ten lanes wide, cars bumper to bumper, smog, riots, and something called Sig Alerts that Freemont kept going on about but never fully explained. And all that red carpet, gay pride, hair tossing, pink poodle, L.A. bullshit Lougie didn't think he could handle. Boots without holes, jeans with or without, and a barber who understood how to trim a mullet was all you needed. He had his own thing—cool job, driving the tow truck, latest slick gig, and so what if the girls he met lived in trailer parks off Old Nogales Highway. Arizona would do just fine, man.

He said, "No, listen, dude, it's cool. See I get an order to repo a car. Get the make, model, VIN, dude's home address, phone number, place of business, they give me all that. I drive around, watch and wait, and when the timing's right I pull a 'back and grab.' I told you what that was, didn't I?"

Lougie made a left through an opening in the median and crossed into the K-Mart parking lot, wide-open and empty this time of night.

Fremont said, "That's where you snatch the car by the front with hydraulic forks, huh?"

"Takes fifteen, maybe, twenty seconds at the most. Guy can be standin' in a phone booth, by the time he hears the commotion and tells the other person on the line 'Hang on a second,' you're a half-block down the street and gatherin' speed."

Fremont said, "Man, and you get…what?…eight-nine dollars an hour for your time? Shit!"

Lougie drove the rig out to a spot in a far corner of the lot, off away from the K-Mart building. There he tucked the phone to his shoulder, clutched the truck into reverse and began backing. The truck made a *dooot…dooot…dooot…*warning sound, as he angled the truck and Mercedes into one of the slots. Lougie said, "Ten…" braking into the space, "but here's where the cool part comes in. See…I don't take the car to the impound lot like I'm supposed to. Instead I drop it someplace. Then I call the guy, the car's owner, on the phone and say, 'Hey, I just repo'd your car, dude, but if you want it back, I can tell you where it's at for a hundred dollars.'"

"Hundred dollars, huh?" Fremont said, seeming a little more interested now.

"Yeah, dude says, 'That's bullshit!' and I say, Fine! I'll just take it to impound where you'll have to come up with the last six months car payments and the impound fees to get it back. Man, the dude always pays."

Lougie waited for Fremont to respond, picturing him running it through his mind, the way it would work.

Fremont said, "Yeah, dude pays, you still get your ten bucks an hour."

"And a week later," Lougie said, "the dude gets careless, one of the other tow drivers picks it up again."

"Not bad, my man. But it's still chump change. You know what I'm saying?"

Lougie felt his mood sink a bit, but he let it go. His buddy could talk that way now that he was rich. He still thought he had a cool thing going, and he could tell Fremont was reasonably impressed. He ended the call, saying he'd catch him later.

At one a.m., Lougie found a pay phone and placed the call, using the number from the repo order on his clipboard. He was cool, careful not to call from his cell phone, so there was no record of the call that could be traced back to him. "A sleepy headed guy answered the phone and Lougie said, "Hey, man, I just repo'd your car."

"What?" the sleepy voice said.

"I said I just repo'd your car, dude."

"Just a minute," the guy said.

There was a long pause as Lougie waited.

The guy came back on saying, "No you didn't!"

"What?"

"No you didn't," the guy said. "I can see it in the driveway!"

Lougie, reading from his clipboard said, "Are you Robert Chatsworth."

"Yeah...?"

Lougie said, "Shit!" and hung up the phone.

If he hadn't repo'd Chatsworth's car at 4740 West Snyder, then whose car had he...?

It suddenly hit him. The houses off Craycroft, where he snagged the black Mercedes, were in the *East* numbering scheme—not West. He'd looked for the house number and the make of car. Finding a black Mercedes there, he saw no reason to compare the registration number to the license plate on the car.

Lougie got back into his truck and ground it into gear. He pointed the truck, west, toward home, and kept his foot in it all the way. It was a story he'd tell Fremont, maybe, someday over a cold brew, if he got the chance. But for now, he just wanted to get home. He was dealing with a cold hard fact—he'd just snagged the wrong car, stolen it, some might say.

*   *   *   *

Jana Layman usually remembered one outstanding detail about each of the men she'd killed. The drug dealer in Phoenix had lacquered fingernails he had put on in a salon. She'd taken sixty thousand off the dude and left him dead in the parking lot behind the club, the engine to his big pimpmobile still running. Randy the commodities broker, who kept money he scammed from his firm—ninety-five and change—in the engine compartment of his yacht, wanted to be called *Captain Randy*. And the gumba, Richie, her latest, had a collection of Barbie dolls, one or more of which he'd select to take to bed with them whenever they had sex. What? Did he fantasize they were having a threesome?

Each of the men she'd set-up to kill and rob had their quirks, but what they all had in common was they were all assholes the world would be better off without. She made that her number one criteria in deciding whom to hit. Each had acquired their wealth through illegal means, and each held much of their assets in cash. That was what Jana looked for. Follow the scent of *sweaty money*, she told herself. That's the trail to success.

It had started with the Libyan College boy, back while she was still with the Corp. The young, nappy-haired guy had been the objective of her last assignment with Marine Corp Intelligence. And looking back, it had been the genesis of her new profession.

The assignment was at a University in Frankfurt, Germany, where a small, tight-knit group of Libyan males were attending as students. Her mission was to get close to the group and monitor their activities for subversive behavior. In particular, Raj Al Akmed, the son of a high-ranking Libyan official, who was suspected of having links to terrorist groups throughout the Middle East. "The Raj" as he called himself, was just a spoiled rich kid as far as Jana could see, but her government, for whatever political motive, wanted someone inside with him.

"He like's American girls," her C.O had said. "In particular, small blondes with big racks."

Jana fit the mold, she had to admit: a five-two, hundred-and-eight pound knockout, and stacked. She was at ease with herself, her looks, the startling affect it had on men. Still, she resented the way her C.O.—all of them—saw her. Eleven missions behind enemy lines, six confirmed kills as a forward insurgent, and all they could see was her cup size. But in the Corp, orders were orders. You didn't question them. In the fall, she began classes as Susan Gail Brown.

For the next six months, into second quarter, Jana played *Susie Co-ed*, getting close to The Raj and his pals, and reporting all details of their movements and associations. Of particular interest to the Pentagon was how Raj spent his money. It would mean getting to know Raj on an intimate level. Was she comfortable with that? "Fuck the guy, you mean?" Jana had said to her C.O. "Does it matter if I'm comfortable or not?"

No it didn't, and so she did, the first night into their relationship, and once, some times twice, a night thereafter. Something she accepted and performed for—moaning and cooing as The Raj grunted out his seed.

The act, repulsive as it was to her, reminded her of survival training. A whole lot like eating grubs, she decided. Something no one in his or her right mind would find pleasant. Just something you had to grit your teeth for and do. Yes, it meant fucking one of Libya's new elite, but what it also meant was getting stoned-to-the-zone at off-campus Rave parties and spending mindless nights getting sloshed in college bars with a bunch of towel heads. They were the most boring pack of assholes she'd ever encountered, and the way Raj spent his money, from what she could see, was buying Ecstasy to trade for sex with college girls. He always had loads of cash.

The official mission ended in early spring, when dialogue between the U.S. and Libya resumed, and orders came to return to Camp Lejeune. But Jana's experience with The Raj and his buddies was anything but over.

On her last night in Frankfurt, their farewell celebration, Raj slipped Jana a roofie. For more than four hours, Raj and his buddies took turns with her on the backseat of her rented car, leaving her to wake alone in the deserted hours of morning with only dreamlike recollections of what had transpired.

That morning, sore and bruised, her normally bright eyes dull and buried in circles of black, Jana caught-up with Raj near his apartment as he was taking a shortcut through the alley toward the Ald Stöt. She shot Raj between the eyes with her service revolver, and with even less remorse than those she'd taken down in the line of duty. For measure, she lifted two grand from his person and made it out of there without being seen. She caught her military hop at Ramstein and made it out of the country.

Given the classified nature of her association with the young Libyan, the entire incident was swept under the Pentagon's carpet. The matter was enough, however, to earn her a discharge and a ticket home to Benson, Arizona.

There, she found herself a civilian for the first time in eight years. All she had to show for her military service was six credits in economics, a sore crotch, and the ability to kill a man with guns or knives—take your pick.

What was a single girl to do?

The answer came to her without the question being asked…Do what you do best, girl…use your significant feminine gifts to get close to men with money, then blow their fucking brains out at close range and take it.

Three in the morning, Jana sat smoking and drinking coffee in an IHOP on Grant Road. Christ! She'd fucked up good this time, unlike the previous two, the drug dealer in Phoenix and the Commodities Broker—fucking crook—in Corpus Christi—those had gone exactly as planned, a precision drill that she had executed to the letter, leaving no trace of herself behind. But tow truck drivers—Christ!—how did you plan for that?

Out there somewhere was a car with a dead body, two hundred thousand in cash, and her purse…like a Goddamn public service announcement: "Your killer is Jana Layman."

Shit!

She had caught the name of the tow service, A-1 Towing, from the door panel of the truck. And she had glimpsed the driver: a yerkel with a ratty mustache and a stupid grin on his face—a guy making minimum wage to fuck up her plans. She didn't believe he'd seen her. She had to think.

There were two options, the way she figured: get the hell out of town, tonight, do it! Or try to find out what happened to the car. There was a chance—God, say there was a chance!—that the car had not been gone-over at the impound. She could imagine it tucked amid thousands of other impounded cars and trucks, a sea of them, and maybe, just maybe, the body, the money, and her purse had not been discovered. In which case, maybe she could coo the lot owner into letting her retrieve some things from it...well, the purse and money anyway, the body she'd have to leave behind. And God—God!—she'd have to be careful.

*   *   *   *

Lougie spent the night tossing and turning. At the very least his little fuck-up could cost him his job; at best someone could be reporting the car stolen this very minute. Did anyone spot him towing the car? Could he explain his actions away? Maybe if he'd returned it right away or called his supervisor, got Arnold out of bed and excused the mistake as soon as he realized...

But he hadn't. He had hesitated, become frozen with indecision. Damn! Now it was too late. How did he explain driving the car miles out of the way, in the opposite direction from the impound lot? Dropping it in the lot? He could return to the car and find some identification; call the owner, straighten things out.

Lougie stewed into the wee hours of morning, falling asleep at last then sleeping longer than he'd wanted to. He drove out Broadway to the K-Mart, but by the time he got there, ten-thirty or so, the lot was already filled with cars—Blue-Light shoppers coming and going. At least the car, the black Mercedes was still there, off in the corner, in the shade of the fan palms. Maybe the owner hadn't noticed it missing yet.

Lougie pulled his tow truck along the edge of the lot nearest Broadway and sat watching the car. He could back-and-grab it, tow it to the desert, but risk, even further, being seen and associated with the car. As it was, there was a chance no one had seen his A-1 Tow Truck last night, in which case he might already be off the hook. It was a chance.

He could walk over there, take a look.

Lougie sat studying the car. If the doors were unlocked, maybe he could sneak a peek at the registration. But what if the car had been reported stolen and the cops were sitting back somewhere among the other parked cars, watching to see what happened?

Lougie scanned the lot for suspicious looking cars, guys in dark glasses. He didn't see any, but...

Shit! You always wimp out on things like this, he told himself. You know you do. If Fremont were here, he'd say, "Damn, man, just walk on over, ain't no one gonna notice." Fremont, that way, would do it. Get into his walk and just slide over there, cool. But Lougie wasn't Fremont, and Fremont wasn't here. And, shit, he was wishing just now that he'd taken Fremont up on his suggestion and moved to California.

Lougie put the truck in gear, eased toward the entrance, then pointed the truck out and west on Broadway. "Leave it be," he told himself. He would take his chances.

✳   ✳   ✳   ✳

Jana arrived at the impound yard. It was strung with chain link and razor wire, and there was a small shack near the gated entrance. The lot manager had heavy brows and a low, sloping forehead that gave him a kind of Neanderthal look. An embroidered patch on his coveralls said his name was *Arnold*. He stood inside the door of the shack, clipboard in-hand, watching her as she drove in through the gate.

Talking to her breasts, Arnold told Jana that they hadn't *brung* in any black *Mercedes* last evening, but maybe it was one of the other yards. She told him, No, no...She was pretty sure it had been A-1, could he check again.

Scanning his clipboard, he said, "Huh-uh...ain't no record of it. But you're free to look around you want." She nearly expected him to add, *"both of you,"* As his eyes returned to her breasts once more.

There were cars of all makes and models in the lot, most damaged in some-way. There was a black Mercedes similar to the gumba's, but the entire left front quarter panel had been ripped away, and there was a head-sized, starburst pattern in the windshield on the passenger side. Jana made her way up one row and down another, weaving her way between the stacks of cars and piles of auto parts. Not finding Richie's Mercedes, she returned to the impound shack, where Arnold was still watching.

"Satisfied?" he said.

Jana opened the door to her car and got one foot inside, but paused leaning her arms on the doorframe. "Hey, Arnold, how many drivers you got on at night?"

Arnold seemed to think hard about it, count on his fingers, and think some more, before saying, "One!"

Jana smiled, formed a slender forefinger into a gun, and shot Arnold once with it. He liked that; she could tell by the toothless grin he was hanging onto as she slid behind the wheel. Only one possible driver, Jana thought, as she backed the car out through the open gate...how hard could it be?

*   *   *   *

It was dark—way dark—west of town, outside the glow of city lights. Snake-back Road, off Kinney, leading out to the impound lot, made a twisting loop through nothingness-desert before hooking up with Kinney again two miles farther out. There the road led off west to more nothingness and the barren Avra Valley, where nighttime temperatures could hover above ninety, and where no one wanted to live.

Lougie wheeled the tow truck, windows down, through the dips and curves, feeling the hot desert air wash through the cab. Saguaro and cholla cacti formed shadowy stick figures outside the sweep of his headlights. He was delivering his first haul of the night out to the impound lot—a late model Ford Fiesta that was four months overdue on payments.

He had decided against pulling his scam on this owner, still nervous about the Mercedes that, last check, still sat in the corner of the K-Mart parking lot. It was quiet out here, the desert always silent, and it made him think of his buddy Fremont.

He pictured him in his beach house in Malibu, his smoking jacket, looking like the black man's answer to Hugh Hefner. He was out there on a sofa, Lougie imagined, amid a dozen sexy girls in skimpy bikinis and transparent beach wraps. The bunch of them drinking Couvossiere and smoking weed; the girls hanging on every word Fremont spoke—all that jive—and laughing. It made him feel lonely. He was thinking too much, feeling sorry for himself, and believing that maybe—just maybe—Fremont was right, he should go west.

Coming out of a dip, his headlights caught first a glimpse of car—a Dodge Intrepid, hood raised, on the shoulder—then fell flush across a girl in the road. She was wearing tight, Daisy Duke cut-offs and a halter top with—Christ!—full breasts spilling out where loosened tie strings were supposed to cinch them in.

She was barefoot, her sandals dangling from one hand, and had a thumb raised to traffic. His first thought: Holy shit!

Lougie clutched and down shifted, feeling the car on back wanting to fishtail. He hit the brakes hard and put the entire rig into a power slide and brought it to a stop, only yards in front of her.

Now he watched as she came around the front, padding on tiny, delicate feet.

"Hey, Cowboy!" she said, as her face appeared inside the rolled-down window. "How about a lift back to town?"

Christ!

Fremont and his ladies completely forgotten, Lougie unhitched the Ford Escort and left it beside the road—someone else's problem. He hitched, in its place, Jana's Intrepid and found a sandy flat in which to turn the rig around and point it back toward town.

On the drive, she told him thanks, she'd been looking for a shortcut to the Freeway when her car had broken down, absolutely sure it was the damned transmission. He told her Chryslers were notorious for that, asked, "You want to hear some music?"

They were quiet for a while, Sweet Home Alabama playing from the radio, Lougie stealing glances at this gift from heaven—her thighs, her breasts, the blonde hair that billowed over her shoulders. As the song ended, he took a chance, said, "Hey, you wanna get high?"

Lougie produced a joint from his coverall pocket and they toked it together, holding the smoke in their lungs, saying things like, "Oh yeah," and "Sweet!" as they exhaled.

Later he asked, "You hungry? I can stop off 'the Burger King?"

The hot little mind-blower turned to lean against the door. She pulled one bare leg up next to him on the seat. "You wouldn't want to ruin my buzz, would you? I thought we were having fun."

A bare foot came to tease at Lougie's hip; a sly smile teased at the girl's lips.

"You're somethin', you know it?" Lougie said, touching his tongue to his lips. Suddenly everything in his mouth had gone dry.

"Yeah? And just what kinda 'something' would that be?" Her toes teased.

"I got a bottle," Lougie said, ideas for things to say coming hard. "Want a drink?"

The girl came off the door now to slide across the seat next to him. She got close, right up against him, put one arm across his shoulder, and let the fingers of her other hand trail lightly across his chest. She spoke into his ear when she said,

"Bring it on Cowboy. I'm in a mood to party." Her voice had become a sultry whisper.

Lougie used his free hand to pinch himself, make sure he hadn't dozed off behind the wheel. He was aware of a painful ache in his groin and a sudden tightness in his jeans.

They sipped from the bottle, taking turns, as the girl's hand slid purposefully up and down his thigh. He was surprised that this beautiful girl would come sit close to him, surprised by everything she did. It was miles from the norm for him, and he had to concentrate hard to keep the truck on the road.

They had nearly polished off the bottle by the time they came out of the darkness of desert and into the lights of town. Lougie had yet to ask this girl her name, and she had yet to ask his. But here she was—Thank you God!—with her slender fingers conducting a symphony along his thigh. Lougie glanced down into the bottomless abyss between her breasts, the tight juncture of her thighs. His loins were at a popping point and he fought to hold onto himself. He put himself out there once more, this time saying, "You have a place to stay tonight?" And was surprised once again as the girl put her lips to his ear, and flicked her tongue softly inside. It was wet and warm, and the waves that rolled through his groin were almost more than he could stand.

"I do, if you do," she said.

The words, whispered softly in a warm rush of breath, were all that he could bear. Lougie squeezed his eyes tight and gripped the wheel, as a lightening bolt hit his groin, and release came wet and warm. He felt a stain spread through his jeans, beneath her hand; he felt bliss, the likes of which he'd never known, and at the same time shame the depths of which he'd never before fallen. He rocked against the back of his seat, fighting to keep the truck between the lines. As he came around, the girl patted his leg. "Don't worry, Cowboy," she said. "We've got all night."

That's the way Lougie came to know Jana Layman. He would remember this night, in days to come, as the luckiest fucking night of his life.

*   *   *   *

Breakfast the next morning they were across a booth from each other at Denny's: Lougie with the country fried steak and eggs, Jana with black coffee and a pack of Winstons.

She studied Lougie through the cloud of smoke that drifted up from the cigarette she kept poised at her lips, thinking the man ate the way he made love—like he had a fire to go to.

Last night, humping her every hour or so, he would use the rest pauses between to tell her about his life, his work, something on his truck called a 'back and grab.' But mostly he talked about his friend—some black dude named Fremont. He told her how they would hang together; how they had worked as janitors, for a time, cleaning office buildings; how they had gone to work for a developer, a mob guy who was now drooling in his food after some kind of stroke; and how the buddy, Fremont, who reminded Lougie of Martin Lawrence only taller and thinner, had moved away to California, leaving Lougie without much of anyone to talk to. This morning, the dynamo finally out of steam, apparently had nothing left to say.

Jana smoked and watched Lougie using his toast to shovel hunks of steak and runny eggs into his mouth. The question on her mind: What had the yerkel done with Richie's car? If it wasn't at the impound, where had he taken it? And why? Had he discovered the money, the two-hundred-thousand beneath the seat? Had the cops discovered the body? She didn't think so. She had watched the early news and heard nothing reported. And if this tow-pilot had found the money, he would be busting at the seams to tell someone.

So how to approach the subject?

Jana asked, "You been driving a tow truck long?"

Lougie, with a mouth full of grub and stuffing more in, shrugged. "Couple of months."

Okay, a start. She said, "So you like it?"

"I guess."

"You guess? It seems like a pretty sweet gig to me. Drive around all night. No boss looking over your shoulder."

"Yeah, that part's okay."

Jesus! Getting this guy to open up was like stacking sand; you had to keep at it. Jana drew on her cigarette and blew the smoke from the corner of her mouth. She said, "I've been wanting to ask. Last night you dropped that car in the desert without a second thought. Weren't you afraid you'd get in trouble?"

Lougie carved off a chunk of breaded steak and sopped it in his gravy before stuffing it into his mouth. "Long as no one saw me take it."

He went on eating, but seemed to consider the idea, mental cogs meshing slowly, as the picture of it came into his mind. He said, "Maybe I'll call the owner later, let him know where to find it. Sometimes they're so happy to just get the car back they don't make a stink about it."

She said, "You've done this before, tow a car and not take it back?"

Lougie put his fork down and leaned forward on his elbows. He took a quick conspiratorial glance over his shoulder, before saying, "Can you keep a secret?"

Bingo! They were getting to it now. Jana snubbed out her cigarette and pushed the ashtray aside to lean in. She said, "I love secrets. Tell me."

"Well…" Lougie said. He paused as a waitress came around with coffee and refilled their cups. When she'd gone, he said, "I got this really cool scam."

Lougie laid it out for her. He told her how he'd devised this scheme of extorting money from car owners who were late with their payments. Gave her the whole routine, now, seeming anxious to tell someone, anyone. The big genius, proud he'd hatched the idea in his own pumpkin head.

Jana feigned wide-eyed interest, appearing to hang on every detail. He finished by saying, "I don't know, I guess it's not such a big deal. My friend Fremont still thinks I'm working for peanuts."

"Was that who you were talking to on the phone this morning while I was in the shower?"

"Yeah, we stay in touch."

"Well," Jana said, "I've never met this Fremont, but you want to know what I think? I think that's the most perfect scam I've ever heard."

Lougie said, "I guess…" then nearly guffawing, added, "but you really need to make sure you get the right car."

And there it was.

This guy, Lougie, pulled repos and made extra bread by extorting the owner. But this time—this one time—he had snagged the wrong car by mistake— Richie's car. Realizing, he panicked and dropped the car someplace to get rid of it—dumb yerkel, dumb luck. Christ! And now she was staring at *Life Without*.

Jana's first reaction was to reach across the table, grab the hayseed by the throat and squeeze. Where? You fucking moron! Where's the car?

But she didn't. She kept her cool.

Jana put on her best look of incredulity, said sweetly, "No! No way! That can't happen! Can it?"

Lougie said, "Not only can…Did!"

*   *   *   *

In the tow truck, Jana sat close with her hand on Lougie's thigh. The guy was easier to lead than a bug on a string, though, in a head-to-head, standardized test comparison, she believed the bug would prove to have the higher IQ.

She had convinced him, at the table, to show her the car. "Come on, I want to see it!" she had said, giving him a glimpse of cleavage and a little girl show of interest. "Later you can show me how that back-and-grab thing works, maybe teach me how to do one."

The bubble of hope that had swelled in Jana at the coffee shop suddenly burst as they pulled into the K-Mart parking lot. The car was there, but Jesus look at it.

The Mercedes sat in the corner of the lot, where Lougie had said it would be, but instead of gleaming in the noonday sun, it was a wreck.

"Oh, my God!" Jana said. "What happened?"

Jana slid from the tow truck and crossed to where the car sat in the shade of fan palms. The windows had been busted out, all the way around, and every square inch of the deep metallic black had been spray painted over with elaborate colorful gang graffiti.

Inside, her purse was missing, along with her wallet, credit cards, driver's license, and the gun she'd used to snub Richie. The bag of cash, stuffed hurriedly beneath the seat, was missing also. Jana wasn't sure whether to rejoice or vomit. On one hand, all the evidence linking her to the car and Richie's body had vanished, on the other hand, she had just seen two-hundred-thousand-dollars disappear on the wind. Money she'd worked and planned for months to acquire— gone.

She stood shaking her head at the graffiti. She could picture some little taggers trashing the car for kicks, then coming across her purse and thinking they'd hit it big. Then she pictured them finding the bag of cash, two-hundred-thousand-dollars, stashed beneath the seat, and imagined them dropping to their knees there in the lot to thank Joseph, Mary, and Jesus, and anyone else who would listen, for their amazing luck. At least the trunk appeared to have remained untouched.

She felt Lougie appear at her side.

"Man-oh-man-oh-man! It was okay the last time I checked it. I know it was. Man-oh-man-oh-man-o-man!"

Jana said, "Let's just get out of here, okay?"

*   *   *   *

That night, Jana asked Lougie to leave her alone for a while, would he just leave her?

He said he didn't understand. Why was she mad at him?

"I just need to think," she said, taking the bottle of Jack Daniels and joint he'd rolled for her onto the back porch where it was dark and quiet.

There were stars above. The faint barking of a neighbor's dog could be heard somewhere off in the distance. She sat on the top step with her knees gathered to her, alternately drawing ragged smoke into her lungs and chunking down mouthfuls of whiskey.

The evening news had reported the discovery of a body, identified as one Richie Cavo, in the trunk of a car in an eastside K-Mart shopping center—the Pima County Sheriff's Department stumbling onto what they called an abandoned vehicle. The Deputy being interviewed said they had no specific suspects in the case, and were, for now, calling it a gang related homicide. She was off the hook.

Jana saw it as a chance to start over. But doing what? Christ! Things with Richie had not gone as planned. It put a scare into her. Worse yet, she was wondering: Where would she go? What would she do? Fuck, work in an office? All she knew was being a soldier, and that was no longer an option.

Lougie came onto the porch, too stupid to stay gone for long. He said, "You okay?"

Jana patted the step next to her. She was feeling empathy for the lug, more than she would have normally, and it surprised her. "Come on. Have a seat," she said, handing him the pinched doobie as he slumped down beside her.

They sat, taking turns with the joint, both staring off at the stars. She was barely aware of his presence, when Lougie, sometime later, said, "I got a call from my boss. He told me I was fired."

Jana's head swiveled sharply toward him.

Lougie said, "Not the Mercedes. The Ford Escort we left sitting out on Snakeback Road. I gotta return the tow truck."

Jana said, "Oh," and turned her mind away once more.

She was thinking about the men she'd killed, picturing each of them in vaguely different ways, remembering the commodities broker, Captain Randy, with his little yachting cap pulled low across his eyes, trying to look like a serious seaman; the surprise on the gumba's face, just before she shot him. "What's this shit?" he might have said, if she'd given him the chance. Good God! She had to find a new line of work. Get out of the *black widow* business. Get out for good...

She became aware of Lougie once more—Lougie talking, for how long now? She wasn't sure. But he was talking about his friend Fremont again, saying something about maybe taking off for L.A., something more about Fremont continuously bating him into coming, Fremont calling California the land of opportunity...

"You should go," Jana said.

"You wanna come with me?"

"No...no, I don't think so. I don't know what I'm going to do," Jana said. "But you should go, really. The change might do you good."

Jana went back to staring at the stars, half listening to Lougie, as she questioned what the next step in her life should be—pick another mark and get back to work or find some simple-ass job and go straight. Heads or tails.

The answer would come to her slowly at first, then all at once. Lougie was saying, "Maybe so, it sure worked out for my buddy Fremont. Here's a guy without a dime to his name. Moves to California, gets a job cleaning carpets. Before you know it, he scores two-point-eight million dollars. Keeps most of it in ready cash."

Jana heard the words: *million and cash.* She looked at Lougie and said, "This friend of yours...Fremont...he's rich?"

"Yeah," Lougie said, "no shit. Lives in a beach house in Malibu. Keeps telling me I should come out and live with him."

Jana had to pinch herself to keep from leaping off the steps. She squelched her enthusiasm, taking time to say, "Well, then it's settled. You should leave tomorrow."

"Right after I return the tow truck," Lougie said, then sat quiet for a moment, staring at his boots, before saying, "You sure you don't want to come with me?"

"You know what?" Jana said, putting her arm around Lougie's shoulder. "Maybe I should. If you'll have me, I think I'd like that a lot. You think I'll get the chance to meet this friend of yours?"

"Sure. He's cool. I know he'll like you," Lougie said.

Jana wanted to say: *I'm counting on it.* But she didn't. Instead, she put her face to the warm night breeze and sucked in all the air she could hold.

Lougie said, "You feeling okay now?"

Jana let her breath out in a rush.

She said, "I feel great!"

And why not? she thought...there was suddenly the smell of sweaty money in the air.

ONE DAY AT A TIME

It was like her to be late, Glen Daniels thought, checking his watch against the clock above the bar. Debbie Polanski, one of the most infuriating and silly twits Glen had ever known. Take it easy, Glen told himself. *Clean and sober one hundred eighty-seven days, now, and exactly the kind of thinking you can't afford. Don't blow it.*

From his seat in the corner booth, Glen watched the regulars downing their drinks. A few were cheerful. Most were solemn and angry looking. Mean drunks, the kind he used to be. *"Go on, let go, asshole, you can have just one. You can handle it..."*

But he couldn't handle it; he knew that. Six months into recovery, this night was about following the program. It was about *step nine* and making amends. It was about Debbie, about the deplorable treatment of her. And it was about getting on with getting well.

They had dated for three months last winter, prior to his checking himself into rehab. Debbie had latched on to him at the bar one night. Seeing him, perhaps, as a cause, lost enough to be worthy of her love. Him sizing her up as one of those stupid broads you could talk into anything. A girl who would go out on a freezing, windy night to fetch a fresh bottle of gin, then give head with her coat and boots still on while you drank it. *"Do you love me, Glenny?"* Christ! He never gave her time to wipe her mouth, much less let her feet thaw, before dismissing her home for the night. *"Hey, make sure I get up in time for work, okay?"* Sure, yes, of course, there she'd be, outside his door, bright and early next morning, two steaming cups in hand. He'd take his through the chained opening, leaving her to drink hers on her way out. He had treated her like trash.

She arrived a full thirty minutes late. By then Glen's hands were twisted into sinewy knots. Scratches had appeared on his watch crystal from his constant tapping.

"Glenny!" Debbie said, spotting him from the doorway. She was standing there, done up for her role as martyr, in mittens and a wool coat that hung to her ankles. She was clutching her handbag in both hands, guarding it, like she'd walked all the way from Rose Point through mean streets to get here—a girl in need of an escort, a girl in need of someone, Glen thought. He braced himself for what he expected might be a scene. But, no, she was waving to him now. Debbie Doormat, willing to forgive all and be forgiven, smiling as she came to him. Glen rose politely to greet her.

"What, no hug?" Debbie said.

Reluctantly, Glen leaned the distance between them to give her a quick squeeze. She felt slight in his arms, vulnerable, the way he remembered. She held on when he tried to straighten.

"I knew you would call, someday," she said. "I've always known."

Glen untangled himself. "It's not what you're thinking, Debbie. Can we just talk?"

"So businesslike. Sounds to me like some little boy is having a bad day."

"Deb…"

"Sit, sit," she said, patting the bench where he'd been waiting.

Glen took a deep breath and reminded himself once again why he'd come. Just get this thing done and get out, he told himself. That's all you have to do.

Glen eased into the booth. Debbie slid in across from him. He waited while she removed her mittens and shrugged her coat.

"Debbie…"

"You look good, Glen. You know that? Better than the last time I saw you."

"I've filled out a bit since I took up eating. Listen, Deb…"

"The very place we met, right over there at the bar. I ordered a Martini and you said you were surprised, you expected I'd order a Shirley Temple. Remember that?"

He'd asked himself, earlier, why she'd chosen a bar of all places in which to meet. Predictable irony? Vindictiveness? No, of course, it had been out of sappy sentimentality—Christ! He said, "Yeah, I remember. Deb…"

"All the way over I was thinking about the night we drove out to the Little League Park. That was some night. We made love right on the pitcher's mound."

"Made love?" Glen said. "Debbie, that night I made you do things. Deplorable things. Things that must have been humiliating for you."

"Not humiliating…exactly. Base, perhaps. Crass, yes. But in the spirit of giving, I chose to do them for you. Isn't that what love is all about?"

"No, it's what abuse is all about, Deb. And anger. And insecurity. I've learned that. That's why I asked you here."

"Glenny, don't be shy. It's okay to admit you've been missing me."

"No, Deb, listen…"

"We had such good times. I must have said 'I love you' a thousand times."

She had a dreamy look in her eyes.

"You know, that's probably true," Glen said. "But didn't it strike you a little odd that I never once said it back?"

"That's because you're the strong silent type, silly. But that's okay, I said it enough for the both of us."

Glen felt the old familiar tug at the pit of his stomach; he was starting to need a drink—bad. The sounds of the bar—the voices, the laughter, the clinking of ice inside the glasses—they combined in a lyrical seduction that called to him to join in. His skin began its crawl, as if slowly working itself off his limbs.

"I think I need to get out of here," Glen said.

"You okay? You don't look so good. We could go back to my place. I'll introduce you to aroma therapy."

Glen needed an escape plan. Her place was out of the question, too much time alone with her on the drive out to Rose Point. His place was in walking distance, but then, shit, he'd never get rid of her.

"Let's just go out to your car," Glen said. "We'll talk for a minute and then you can go, alright?"

The art of making amends wasn't turning out to be quite as simple as Glen had estimated. Debbie was making it difficult. Glen's seventeen-year alcoholic rampage had left behind its share of road kill, for sure. But there had been no *deer in the headlights* more deserving of being run down than Debbie. She was the victimizer's victim, a celebrity shoe wipe. The girl—Jesus!

But that was not the point.

The point—his AA friends continued to remind—was that the alcoholic finger of blame always points away from, never toward, the one with the drink in his hand. If he was to continue this touchy dance of twelve-stepping to sobriety, he would have to ignore Debbie's grating personality and put the sole weight of responsibility for his past, and present, behavior squarely on his own shoulders. It was the right thing to do. His challenge, Glen was now coming to understand, would be to simply get the stupid twit to shut-up for five lousy minutes.

Her car was parked at the far corner of the parking lot, freezing when they got there. Glen warmed his ears by rubbing them with gloved hands. Debbie started the engine and got the heater going. As they waited for it to warm-up, Glen watched the blinking neon signs in the window of the bar, out there across the rows of cars. He couldn't take his eyes off them.

"You could warm a girl up," Debbie said.

"What?"

"Come on, silly, put your arm around me, my teeth are chattering."

Reluctantly, Glen lifted his arm and Debbie slid in, nuzzling close. She held on, stroking his chest for a time before saying, "The last time we cuddled like this they were playing a salute to the Righteous Brothers."

"How do you remember all that?" Glen said.

"It's in my diary. I recorded every last thing we did. Want to know why I always thought you'd come back into my life some day?"

Glen was afraid to ask, but said, "No, why?"

"Because of a slogan on a billboard."

"A slogan?"

"It was an ad promoting some kind of perfume...Chanel, maybe...it said, 'Love wins, where love will.'"

"Deb, I don't even know what that means, much less what it's got to do with me calling?"

"You have to take it in context. That day you broke up with me...Remember?...You said some terrible things. Called me names that were just awful."

"Deb, I..."

"You told me to get out. You said you didn't love me. Said you never did. Told me not to come back, you never wanted to see me again. I drove home that morning, tears running down my face...and then, I saw it...'Love wins, where love will.' Isn't that absolutely the most prophetic thing you've ever heard?" Debbie relinquished her embrace long enough to look into Glen's eyes. "Don't you see? It was a sign from above."

Across the lot the neon lights pulsed their vulgar suggestions at him. Glen drew away, staying Debbie at arms length. "A sign from above, Debbie? Above the freeway, maybe. It was a billboard sign, goddamn it! A billboard sign. Christ, you're doing it again!"

"Doing what?" Debbie asked. There was genuine amazement in her eyes.

"I'm going," Glen said. "I'm going back into that bar over there and I'm going to get totally shitfaced. And I don't want you to follow me. I mean it."

"Was it something I said? What ever it was, I'm sorry."

Glen turned to the door; his hand found the handle.

"Glen, don't go! I have a drink for you here!"

An overwhelming flood of raw sweet whiskey taste flooded Glen's mouth. A conditioned response, he understood, but powerful nonetheless. His hand paused on the door handle; his tongue moved to clear the taste from his lips. "You have something to drink?"

"In my purse, a flask. Don't go."

Glen eased back into his seat. "Let me see it," he said.

Debbie quickly fumbled in her bag and came out with a silver flask, held it for him to see.

Again, Glen's mouth watered. He said, "That's the one I made you buy and carry when we were together."

Debbie smiled proudly. "Your back-up, you called it. I saved it all this time."

"Give it to me."

"Will you stay?"

Glen snatched the flask from Debbie's hand. He sat back with it, glaring at her, and unscrewed the cap. "You stupid bitch," he said.

"Glen, why are you mad?"

The urge to tip the flask back and drain it was overwhelming. Something held him back. One hundred eighty-seven days clean and sober, six months of painstaking progress. Instead, Glen sat the flask on the dash, laying the cap next to it, and stared at it. Carefully choosing his words, he said, "Listen! I don't love you! Don't you get it! I didn't then. I don't now. Understand? The reason I called, the only reason, was because I've been to rehab. I've been attending AA and I've been straight for over six months now."

Debbie stared at him for the longest time. Tears were welling in her eyes. Her hands were at her face covering her mouth. Glen waited for the breakdown.

"Oh, no...oh, my..." she said, shaking her head in disbelief.

Glen decided not to give her the chance. He said, "It's part of the program."

"You've been in treatment?" she said. Her head still rocked from side-to-side, grappling with the news. "I am such a ninny. You poor baby, I've been so insensitive. Of course! It's all so clear now. No wonder you're upset with me. You've been trying to tell me something important and I've been running at the mouth, going on about our future without the first thought of what *you* might be going through." Tears of sympathy spilled from her eyes and rolled down her cheeks.

"Debbie, it's the Twelve Step program. Step nine says I must make amends…"

If Debbie heard, it didn't show. There was something more like wonderment in her eyes. She said, "Now it all makes sense."

Debbie grabbed Glen and hugged him fiercely. "You're right," she said, her voice cracking. "I have been so stupid."

"No," Glen said, "those things I just said…"

"It all makes so much sense, now, looking back, all coming together." Debbie's wheels spun, weaving golden logic from sentiments of straw. "Your leaving…those things you said…the anger…it was the alcohol talking, wasn't it? Not you."

Glen wanted to believe she was actually getting it this time. Wanted to scream, "Thank you, sweet God! Finally!" But the look in her eyes, that familiar lovelorn bewilderment, still worried him.

"You did it for me?" Debbie said. "Didn't you?"

"What?" Glen said, warning himself to be careful.

"All of it. It was because you really did love me."

"Debbie, have you heard anything I've been saying?"

"You pushed me away, out of love, so you could free yourself of this illness that was coming between us."

"Are you crazy. I've been trying to tell you that I recognize that I treated you badly, and that I was wrong to do so."

"And you've come to show me what a changed man you are. The new Glen and how bright our future must be now."

"Our future? Goddamn it! There you go again! Those rose colored glasses, Christ, how do you manage to get through an intersection? All the lights must look red to you! There is no future! Listen to the tone of my voice!"

Debbie gathered one of Glen's hands in hers, giving him a soulful look. "I'm listening and I understand," Debbie said. "There's a new Glen, but there's also parts of the old Glen that will emerge from time to time. Like now." Debbie squeezed his hand reassuringly. "I just have to learn to recognize which Glen is which."

Glen could feel his anger building—a familiar raw rage that usually emerged halfway through a bender. In those times it would continue to fester, unless and until he could quell it with more drink, or until he picked a fight and someone put his lights out. Sober he wasn't sure what to expect. He eyed the flask again, fighting the taste on his lips. Across the lot the neon beckoned. "I thought I was getting through to you," he said, "but you're still one crazy bitch, you know that."

"Ooops! There he is again. Old Glen," Debbie said. "But it's okay. Now that I know who's who I can forgive you every time, no matter what you say or what you do." Debbie's hand went to her mouth. "Oh my God!"

"What?" Glen said. He was still fighting the urge to grab the flask and down it, hanging on narrowly.

"Don't you see," Debbie said. "The billboard…the prophecy…" Her eyes were filled with amazement. 'Love wins, where love will.' It's all come true."

There was a loud splintering sound inside Glen's head, like that of a tree limb snapping beneath the weight of snow. He lunged at Debbie from across the seat, forcing his full weight upon her. His gloved hands wrapped around her neck, pushed her down, squeezing. He heard her gasp, felt her struggle beneath him. Her frail legs kicked at the seat, the dash, the steering column, the air. He forced his weight harder, wedging her head between the door and the seat. His hands tightened.

Several minutes passed before Glen eased his grip. He waited, watching for signs of life: a twitch of limb, a sudden intake of breath. There was none. Satisfied, he sat back.

Across the lot, a couple exited the bar hand-in-hand. They hurried off on foot, their laughter leaving steam clouds on the air. On the dash, the flask still sat open; the screw cap lay next to it.

Glen took the flask from the dash. He studied it for a time, turning it this way and that. His reflection glinted back at him in the polished silver. Finally he opened the door and poured the contents of the flask on the ground, then tossed the empty container to the floorboard.

Outside the car, Glen took a last look at Debbie sprawled across the seat. Twelve Steps to a life of sobriety, he thought. And now, Step Nine complete. He had made his amends.

Glen closed the car door gently. Turned his collar against the cold and moved off across the lot toward the street. The neon lights in the bar windows called to him, as before. But, now, he ignored them. Clean and sober one hundred eighty-eight days, counting today. Working the program, he thought, silently applauding himself…one day at a time.

ALL THE NEWS
THAT'S WORTHY

The callers voice was soft and seductive. "Kelly?" the voice said.

It was no one Kelly recognized, but for sure a man's voice. She'd taken the call coming off the set. The cameras were dormant, the crew dispersed, her co-anchor, Christopher Raintree, was already in his dressing room. The five o'clock news report for Tuesday the seventeenth over and done. She said, "Yes, this is Kelly Daily. Who's calling?"

"What's new in the news, Kelly?"

"Excuse me?"

"That was a particularly enjoyable piece about the labor strike. I love it when you say, '*This* just in.' I like to think you're speaking directly to me."

"Who is this?"

The caller said, "Of course, 'Breaking news' is my favorite, I have to admit. It gets me very excited. *You!* get me very excited."

"Alright, whoever you are, quit fooling around."

"The way you stay with a police chase for hours" the caller said, "oh, my."

Kelly was trying to decide if it was Brian from the control room. The prankster. He'd been hitting on her for months now, sometimes sending what passed for flirtations across the teleprompter in the middle of her newscast. He might write, "You look tired. Were you up all night thinking about me?" or "What color are your panties?" Hoping to get her flustered on-air, maybe get a rise out of her. She could picture him secreting the phone in the corner, at the back of the control room. Keeping his voice low and snickering. She'd thought him harmless until now.

"Brian is that you? If it is, it's not funny, okay?"

"I particularly enjoyed the story about the homeless man found beaten to death," the caller said. "We need more stories like that one. There's a certain twinkle you get in your eye when you have to report a violent crime. Something you can't seem to suppress. It makes me wonder if you enjoy the rough stuff just a little. Do you, Kelly? Do you like your sex tinged with violence? The news worthy way?"

"I'm calling the police, you sick bastard," Kelly said.

"Don't be upset, Kelly," the voice said, disguised perhaps. Still, it was smooth as butter. "We're a lot alike, you and me. We both enjoy the news, so much."

Kelly ended the call by slamming the receiver. It bounced and rattled in its cradle. She waited, staring at it, expecting it to ring again. She was trembling, she realized, more out of rage than fear.

She was still staring at the phone minutes later when Christopher Raintree came back onto the set, crossing to the hallway that led to the parking garage. He had changed from his suit jacket into a preppy sweater that coordinated with his tie beneath the v-neck opening—a Stanford guy, on his way to the polo club, no doubt. He paused, seeing her there, standing over the backstage phone. "Kelly, you okay?" he asked. She imagined she looked visibly shaken.

Kelly shook herself loose. "Yes, yes, I'm fine," She gave him a weak smile. "Looks like you caught me day dreaming."

"I'm going for a cocktail at the club. Care to join me?"

"No…thank you, though…" she said. She was drifting back in thought to the caller, that smug controlled voice. Was Brian somewhere back there beyond the set, watching?

"Yes, well, if you change your mind, you know where it is," her co-anchor said.

Kelly stayed on the set long after Christopher had gone, watching the phone and waiting for the caller to call back. He didn't. Not until a week later. The day of the brutal rape-homicide.

"Kelly?" The call, this time, came an hour and a half before news time. Kelly was in her office, at the computer, catching up on e-mail. The familiar lyrical tone in his voice made her stiffen.

"Yes?" She sat up, leaning into the phone.

"The news has been a little slow lately," the caller said. "All that Middle East hoopla. Blah, blah, blah. It doesn't do a thing for me. It's…" The caller seemed to consider. "…too impersonal, don't you think?"

"What do you want?" Kelly asked, looking past the glass enclosure of her office, out into the newsroom, seeing if she could spot Brian anywhere.

"I want news, Kelly. Same as you. News that makes me feel something. I want to see that seductive glint in your eye once more. The one you get when the story speaks directly to that tingly little place inside you. That's why I'm giving it to you first, so you can give it the delicate caress it deserves. The breaking news today, Kelly," the caller said, "can be found at the Dreamland Motel, off Sunset. Room seventeen. Don't thank me now. There will be time for that later."

The caller hung up.

Kelly set the receiver back in its cradle and stepped into the hallway. Around the newsroom, people went about their business, unaware. There was no sign of Brian. Then, from the doorway that led to the stairwell, Brian appeared. He swaggered, as he came down the aisle. *He can't help it*, she thought.

He seemed not to notice her at first—his head buried in news copy, whistling as he scanned the pages. When he was directly in front of her, he glanced up, gave her a wink and a grin, and moved on. Kelly watched him swagger on down the aisle and into the control room. When the door swung shut behind him, she returned to her office.

She brooded over Brian, over the call, wondering if she should be concerned. It could all be someone's stupid idea of a joke—*Brian's* stupid idea of a joke. She reached for the phone, deciding to call the station manager. Then changed her mind and went directly to his office.

Bill Thornton bought his suits at the Big and Tall Men's shop, but rarely wore the jacket. Preferring, instead, to turn the cuffs of his shirt back, presenting himself as a hands-on executive.

Kelly remained on her feet, telling Thornton of the caller. Part way into it, he stayed her with a hand. "Hold on a minute," he said and pressed the button on his phone. "Marta," he said into the intercom, "Get Raintree, would you? Pronto!" Turning back to her, he said, "You say this guy has called before?"

"Yes. I'm sure it's the same one. I thought it could be Brian. He's always making obscene overtures. But I can't be sure."

"Brian from Production?"

Kelly nodded.

"Yeah, I can see that, maybe," Thornton said. "He's got a couple of marks against him already, the little shit."

"Are you going to talk to him?"

Before Thornton could answer, Christopher Raintree came through the door, knocking once as he entered. "What's up?" Christopher said, looking from Thornton to Kelly.

Thornton gestured him to a seat. "I want you to hear this," Thornton said. "The two of you are a team."

Kelly related the details of both anonymous calls. She said nothing more about Brian. Still she couldn't help thinking about him—the wink, the sly grin. "What do you think we should do?" she asked when finished, looking to Thornton for answers. "I mean we should have someone check the motel, shouldn't we?"

"It sounds legit enough to, at least, have the police check it out," Thornton said, looking to Raintree now. "Any thoughts to add, Chris?"

"Just one," Christopher said, checking his watch against the news hour, "we roll the news van first."

It was the lead story at the top of the hour. The body of a young prostitute was found brutally bludgeoned in a motel off Sunset. Lantana Jacobs had been laid out on the bed, legs spread. There were signs of forced penetration. Her hands had been carefully positioned, palms-up, the suggestion of invitation to them.

Adrenalin was high inside the newsroom, as airtime approached. A make-up assistant was fretting over sweat beads that refused to leave Kelly's lip. Next to her, at the news desk, Christopher Raintree fiddled with the connection on his lapel mic. "I need water!" Kelly cried. "Can I get some goddamn water?"

"Get her some water," someone responded off set, and a glass was quickly shoved in front of her.

"Take it easy," Christopher said quietly. "Just go with it."

She was fighting a rising sense of despair that began the moment the body was discovered. The live team phoning it in had set the show time madness in motion. There were always pre-air butterflies, sure, but this was something else, Kelly realized. The news had become personal, the way the caller planned it. And a young, black woman was dead, the obvious victim of that sick sonofabitch.

"We're going live in three...two..."

Kelly downed the water, shook back the jitters, and stuffed the glass beneath the news desk.

"...one!

"Good evening," she said, reigning in her nerves, and speaking directly to the camera, "I'm Kelly Daily...

"And I'm Christopher Raintree," her co-anchor interjected.

"...and this is Eyewitness News at five. Our top story today..."

In high school, Kelly was the editor of the student newspaper. After graduation, she worked as a copy assistant, earning her stripes while attending the Columbia School of Broadcasting. She finished her degree, hungry for the big time, and landed a job as a field reporter in Tucson—an entry-level position, covering parades and wildfires, illegal aliens and drug busts.

For two years, she reigned as the local media darling. Her fresh look and cool style won her praise. Raw ambition and guiltless self-promotion drove her forward. She carved her initials into the KTUC news desk as affirmation of where she was headed. News anchor. Nothing less would do. Six months later, Kelly got her shot. And it came in a way she never expected.

In Los Angeles—a coveted market—the patriarch of evening news, Leonard Aston, died of stroke. Surprising the world, Kelly grabbed the slot from under the noses of veteran colleagues, who'd been waiting in line for the old man's job for decades. Bright, witty, beautiful and ambitious, she was media's Golden Girl, and the Los Angeles public loved her. Go after the good stories, she'd told herself, those personal to you.

Now she was getting her chance.

The Homicide Detective appeared in the wings with Bill Thornton, halfway through the news hour. He was a short, pot bellied man in his fifties, with a scraggly little mustache that struggled to reach the corners of his mouth. The sleeves of his suit jacket hung well beyond his wrists. He was not at all what Kelly might have imagined.

The camera bounced between Kelly and her co-anchor. Between cuts, she watched the little man watching them. He seemed to enjoy the newscast, becoming wholly gleeful at what he apparently took for witty repartee—the hand-offs from one anchor to another, the two of them, Christopher and her, working the news effortlessly as a familiar and seasoned team. Finally they signed off.

"...and that's all the news that's worthy," Kelly said, the team's signature line.

"Good night," Raintree concluded.

Someone off camera said, "...and we're out."

Cameras were rolled away and lapel mics were disconnected. Kelly crossed with Christopher to where Thornton and the little homicide detective were waiting.

"You guys are so cool," the little man said.

His voice was a nasal, Chicago accent that called to mind the *Ditka* bit on SNL. She could picture this little man with a plate of pork ribs in front of him, barbecue sauce smeared about his face. Without waiting to be introduced, he removed a badge from his suit coat pocket and showed it to them, saying, "I'm Detective Kazinski. But you can call me Percy. I already know the two of you. You're *fee'mous.*"

"I suppose you want to hear about the caller?" Kelly said.

"I'd like to hear it from the *hoor'sez* mouth, if you don't mind. Not that I think of you as a horse or anything."

Kelly stifled a smile. Despite the circumstances, the man did bring a certain levity to the job.

"Why don't we use your office, Kelly," Thornton said. "Maybe the Detective will want to see where this last call came in."

In Kelly's office, Thornton and Raintree stood by as Kelly related to Kazinski the calls that had preceded the discovery of the body.

The pudgy little detective moved about the room, listening—she guessed— and touching all of her personal effects. "Is that Owen Wilson, the movie star, in the picture with you?" he asked, interrupting her in mid-sentence. He was pointing to a framed photo on the wall above his reach, genuinely star struck.

"No," Kelly said. "That's the Prime Minister of England, Tony Blair. I had a chance to interview him on location in London last year."

"Oh," Kazinski said. "I saw him once at a Starbucks in Burbank."

"Tony Blair?"

"No, Owen Wilson," Kazinski said. "He tried to pretend it wasn't him, but I know it really was. Unless, of course, it was this Tony Blair guy, they look a *lot* alike you know it."

"Can we get back to the caller?" Kelly said. She felt a line knitting its way across her brow.

"Detective," Thornton said, "it's probably worth mentioning that Kelly has had some suspicions of one of our employees, Brian Anderson."

"Brian?" Christopher said, sitting forward. "What's he done?"

"Nothing...really," Kelly said, feeling a bit guilty that she'd directed the finger of blame Brian's way. "He says things sometimes. It's just inappropriate, adolescent behavior. I'm sure of it."

"We should not leave any stone unturned," Detective Kazinski said. He was fingering a particularly delicate clay figurine, now, a souvenir she'd picked up in Cali during a report on the Columbian drug trade.

"I'll have a *tauk* with him, before I leave," Kazinski said through his nose.

Thornton said, "Actually, I think Brian's probably gone for the day, his shift ends immediately after the newscast."

"Tomorrow then, first thing. And we'll want to put a tap on your phone, if that's alright, *Mizz* Daily."

Kelly nodded.

The interview ended.

"It was quite a rush, Kelly," the caller said. "Could you feel it? The girl on the bed, the obscenity...sex sells, Kelly. It makes for very exciting news."

It was later the same evening, Leno was playing on the TV in her bedroom when the phone on the nightstand rang.

"How did you get my home phone, you bastard?"

"It's easier than you might think. Anyone with access to a computer can get it, Kelly. Don't you know that?"

"Why are you doing this?"

"Why, I'm doing it for us, Kelly. To bring us closer together. Actually, I'm feeling very close right now. *Very* close."

Something in the caller's voice sent her to the window. Parting the blinds, she peered down onto the street below. There in the lamplight, the opposite side of the street, a man in a wide brimmed hat and an overcoat waved to her. Kelly jerked away from the window. Putting her back to the wall she drew her bathrobe tighter. "Brian, the police are on to you. They're probably watching you right now."

"You think you know who this is, Kelly. How can I convince you you're wrong?"

"Tell me who you are, that will convince me."

"Yes, I suppose it would," the caller said. "But I have a much more exciting way."

The caller hung up.

They were in her office the following morning, waiting for her to arrive: Detective Kazinski, Bill Thornton, and Christopher Raintree. All were wearing downcast expressions; a technician worked quietly on her telephone. He finished quickly and departed.

"What's going on?" Kelly asked.

"It's Brian," Christopher said, after some hesitation.

"You caught him?"

"Not egg'zactly," Kazinski said. "After your call to us last night, we sent a car to Brian Anderson's apartment. We must'a got there a minute too late. We found him dead."

Kelly felt her head go light. Her knees buckled.

It was Raintree who caught her before she crumpled. He eased her into a chair. "Sit, I'll get you some water."

"I hate to add to your distress," Kazinski said, "But you should know the young man had been decapitated and his head had been displayed atop a broom stick like some kinda standard or something. You have any idea why the killer might do something like that? Maybe some kind of religious rite or something?"

"News worthy," Kelly said.

"What?"

"It's news worthy. Sensational."

Raintree came with the cup of water and Kelly drank it down. Clutching the empty cup in her lap, she said, "His thing is the news. When it gets dull, he makes it more exciting by giving us something bizarre to report on. I think he gets off on it, I don't know."

"Any idea why he chose Brian Anderson?" Kazinski asked.

"It was my fault," Kelly said. "It was all my fault," she was feeling sick. "I was wrongly suspicious of Brian and the caller, this sick fuck, went after him to prove me wrong."

"Why would he want to do that, do you suppose?" Kazinski asked.

"I don't know. Some sense of twisted jealousy, maybe. He said he wants to be closer to me. And it scares the shit out of me, I've got to tell you."

Bill Thornton, had been quiet. Leaning back against her desk, his brow knitted, watching, listening. He came forward now to put his arm around her shoulder. "Don't worry, Kelly. We're all here for you. We're not going to let anything happen to our star."

"Of course not. What would we be without you?" Raintree said.

Kazinski said, "We're going to keep the phone tap active here and at your place of residence. There will be a technician listening in at all times. I don't think you have to worry too much. This guy sounds to me like he's doing these things for you, not to you. But if you go out, take somebody with you. Just to be on the *seefe* side."

They got through the news at five. Raintree displayed the appropriate amount of gravity for the situation. Kelly, herself, could not shield her emotions. She reported the murder of Brian Anderson, one of the stations own beloved news staff, feeling on the verge of breakdown. It was personal to her. *Personal…that word again.*

There were no more calls for the next two days. Kelly stayed close to others. She lunched with one or the other of her co-workers, or took her lunch in. Bill Thornton arranged for a driver to take her to and from work. The investigation continued.

On occasion, Kazinski would pop in unannounced, to say he was working on it. It made Kelly wonder about the man's competency. Still, she was beginning to feel better, having reason to hope the caller had moved on. She wanted to believe that. Or, better yet, believe he'd been accidentally run over by a truck full of scrap metal.

He had not.

On Friday, a week after Brian's murder, the caller made contact again at her office. It was lunchtime and Kelly was eating with her feet propped on the desk. "I'm bored, Kelly," the caller said. "What can I do?"

"You can go to hell," Kelly said, simply.

"Why be terse? You know we're in this together."

"Actually, I do have one suggestion," Kelly said. She imagined a panel truck outside the building, full of surveillance equipment, a police technician in head-phones listening in. She would try to keep the caller talking. She said, "You could come down to the station and give me a face-to-face interview. That would make for some interesting news reporting."

"Very good, Kelly. You're starting to get into the spirit of things. But, no. I have something better planned. More personal.

"I knew Brian. How much more personal can it get?"

"You want a tag line?" the caller said. "How about, 'Eyewitness News *Co-Anchor* Becomes the Latest Victim of Serial Murder.' Would that be personal enough for you? It's certainly sensational."

"God, no! Not Christopher, you sonofabitch! What did he ever do to you?"

The caller hung up.

Kelly quickly got a dial tone and called Christopher's cell phone. When he answered, she told him of the call.

They met in Kelly's office, as before: Bill Thornton coming from his office down the hall; Christopher Raintree returning immediately from lunch; Kazinski, showing from out of thin air.

"I can't deal with this any longer," Kelly told the others. "I feel like I'm going crazy. He's not only killed at least three innocent people that we know of. But now he's threatening Christopher's life."

"We traced the call to a *pee*-phone on Alameda," Kazinski said. But the guy was gone by the time we got there. We're going to send you both to a safe house, until this thing is over."

"Both?" Kelly asked.

Bill Thornton said. "It's a precaution. I've arranged for replacements to handle the newscast for a time."

"But what about the replacements? Won't we endanger them by putting them in our place."

"We don't think so, Missy," Kazinski said. "This *med*-man seems to be focused on you. *Obsessed* if you will. We think he'll start calling to find out what happened to you. We plan to transfer both your office and home lines to the safe house so you can answer. Meanwhile we'll continue to trace and monitor. Maybe this guy will tip his hand along the way. It's a good plan."

Kelly wasn't sure; there was a dull uncertainty nagging at her.

The safe house was a cabin, near Big Bear. Kelly and Christopher Raintree deposited their bags in separate rooms then met with Kazinski one more time before his departure. It was a little after seven. Outside the sky was already dark.

"You have Bobby on the sofa," Kazinski said. And Ree'mend in the car outside. The two will switch-off from time to time to give the *udder* one a *chince* to catch some shuteye."

"I don't know," Kelly said. "I can't help feeling this animal has a way of knowing everything I do. What if he followed us somehow? What if…"

"Then you got Bobby and Ree'*mend*. That's why they're here. Also, there's a three-mile perimeter of harsh land around you, only one access from the highway. The guys will keep an eye on the road. Don't worry. It's a safe house, that's what it is."

Kazinski then made his excuses, before leaving, saying he would stay in touch with them through dispatch. Kelly had to worry, once again, whether, Kazinski, this little man with both the build and dynamics of a fireplug, had a clue in hell what he was doing.

It was sometime after midnight when the phone in the hallway rang. It jolted Kelly out of sleep. She wanted with all her heart to pull the covers over her head and ignore it. But the idea was to take the forwarded calls from her home and office so the technician could trace and monitor them.

As the phone continued, Kelly threw on her robe, wondering to herself why the incessant ringing hadn't brought more activity to the house. Did the others sleep that soundly?

She passed Christopher's room, heading down the dark hallway. The door was closed; no light showed beneath it. In the living room, a full moon shed its glow through the windows. There was no sign of Raymond or Bobby.

The phone continued to ring. Kelly crossed to it, hesitating, taking glances through the windows, trying to spot either or both of the watch-cops about the grounds outside. And Christopher. Why had he not responded to the noise? Finally Kelly answered the phone.

"Kelly?" the caller said.

"What do you want, you sick bastard?"

"Same as always, Kelly. Just more of it."

"Of course…news. Haven't you had enough news already, you've killed three people that we know of, maybe more, just to satisfy your sick perversion."

"I know. You'd think I'd be sated, wouldn't you. But it's kind of like the lyrics to that song. What's it say? something about…da, da, da…'losing all your highs and lows.' Something like that. It just keeps getting more difficult to find that *rush!* You know the one I'm talking about, Kelly. We share it with every news-cast."

"I don't share anything with you, you sick pervert."

Kelly took a quick look down the dark hall toward Christopher's room, still no stirrings. Through the window she could see the SUV they'd used to get here. No sign of Officers Raymond or Bobby.

Kelly prodded. "You said you were going to kill my co-anchor. Just how do you expect to do that?"

"Oh?…Did I say *your* co-anchor?"

A sliver of fear slid between Kelly's shoulder blades. She'd been angry, until now, she realized. Now the dread hand of terror was gently caressing her spine.

The caller said, "You're a co-anchor, too, aren't you, Kelly? You're *my* co-anchor."

She was still trying to reason it when Christopher stepped from the darkness of the hallway and into the room. In one hand he held a gun pointed directly at her. In the other a cell phone to his ear.

"You?"

"Why so surprised, Kelly? We share the news each night, all the news that's worthy. We share the thrill, the exhilaration, the intimacy of it. But it's so hard to keep up the high, don't you think?"

"You can't get away with this, Christopher. The officers...I'm sure they'll be right back."

"I don't think so," Christopher said. "They are no longer."

"The police department's monitoring my phone lines forwarded here. They'll trace the call and know the call came from your cell phone."

"I didn't call your home or your office," Christopher said. "I dialed the line you're talking on direct. The cops won't even know it rang."

"They'll wonder how it is you're the only one left alive."

"A harrowing escape," Christopher said. "Makes for an extraordinary news story, don't you think?"

From the time he'd appeared, they had continued to talk on the phone, face-to-face across the room. Now Kelly lowered the receiver and sat it quietly in its cradle. Still in shadow, Christopher snapped his cell phone closed and crossed into moonlight.

"So what now?" Kelly asked. A strange calm had come over her—maybe weary of the cat and mouse.

"I'm afraid I'm going to have to do despicable things to you, Kelly. Creative things, if I want to outdo my previous efforts. I hope you can appreciate the drama. Can't you see it? A solemn and sob-wracked Christopher Raintree delivers the five o'clock news, alone, to recount the brutal and sadistic murder of his co-anchor, Kelly Daily, the sun that shines on Eyewitness news, no more. Can you picture it? Christ! I get a woody just thinking about it."

"I'll put up a fight," Kelly said.

"I was sure you would. You've always had such a strong life-spark to you, Kelly. That's what I've always loved about you, what brought such exhilaration to our news reports. And it's also why I brought the gun. We'll start with a bullet in the brain."

Christopher brought the gun level with Kelly's eyes. Slowly he thumbed back the hammer and squeezed...

Instead of her skull, the gunshot that boomed inside Kelly's head shattered the window across from Christopher. She had raised her hands at that awful moment, in a futile defensive effort. Now she lowered them cautiously to peer across the top. Christopher still stood in front of her holding the gun, but there was no smoke curling from the barrel. His expression had changed from arrogance to one of surprise and disbelief. He looked first from her to the window, where a jagged hole had been punched through the glass, then back to her once more, before dropping to the hardwood floor.

Detective Kazinski came through the door, his gun at the ready. A young uniformed Rookie charged in behind him, looking to finish the job. But there was nothing to finish. Christopher was dead. *The killer* was dead.

"I was afraid we wouldn't get here in time. I guess we didn't for poor Bobby and *Ree'mend*, we found them outside, one stabbed through the heart, the udder with his throat *sleshed*," Kazinski said.

Kelly was shaking, all the spirit gone out of her. "It was Christopher," she said, "all this time."

"Yeah, we discovered that when we looked back over the phone report. You remember we traced the earlier call today to a phone booth on Alameda. That yielded nothing. We also traced an outgoing call from your office phone, shortly after that, to your co-anchor's cell phone. That was you calling him to warm him of what you thought was a threat on his life. We saw it was his number, at the time, and didn't think much more of it. It was only when we looked more closely at the report, later, that we discovered the global positioning of that cell phone at the time of the call, was the exact same location as that of the phone booth. You caught him on his phone as he was ducking out."

"I'm glad you did," Kelly said. "I have to admit I had my doubts about you. I'm sorry."

"It's okay. I have that effect on people," Kazinski said. "You going to be okay?"

Kelly nodded, though she wasn't sure. What would she do from here? Where would she go? She couldn't go back to being a newscaster; she knew that, not after this. The news had suddenly lost its appeal. She had become the news. And it had become too personal. After all, where on earth could she possibly go now, she thought...to find news this worthy.

"WHO WANTS TO KILL BILLY TINGLE?" (RAISE YOUR HAND)

They came together at Sissy's request—seven women in the parlor with the curtains drawn. They took up space on the sofa, the love seat, or in chairs that had been brought in from the dining room to form a circle. It was the first time they'd met collectively, though all knew something of each other beforehand.

"I think you all know who I am," Sissy said quietly, seeming hesitant at starting things off. She was a frail little woman in her mid twenties—a girl really, compared to the others. Her hands were drawn together in a knot.

"I'm Sissy Tingle," she said. "Billy Tingle's wife. I'm expecting Billy home any minute now, so I only have a short time to say what it is I have to say."

She took a deep breath, and calmed herself. "I appreciate your agreeing to meet this way, but...Oh, this is quite difficult..."

"Stop beating around the bush. Just come out with it, sister."

The response had come from across the circle, from the construction worker named Babe. She was a big woman sitting slouched in her chair. Tattoos and layered fat showed beneath cut-offs and a Spandex top.

Sitting next to her, on the edge of her seat, was the real estate lady, Robin. In contrast, she was neatly dressed in a tan suit, with a stylish red handbag strung from her shoulder. A nametag was pinned to her jacket.

Among the others was Helga, dressed largely in black, storm trooper boots to the knees. Who sat preening coolly, drawing smoke from a brandless cigarette. There was the socialite, Eleanor, dripping diamonds and looking late for the ball. There was a full-figured Hispanic woman, Rosario, her hair teased into a wild Latin Fandango. And there was Marta, the matron, who sat calmly observing the others in a quiet, calculative manner as they waited to hear what Sissy had to say.

Sissy steeled herself and raised her eyes to the circle. "I know all of you have been sleeping with my husband."

The declaration drew anxious glances from some of the women. A bored look from Helga.

"I'd like to hear," Sissy continued, "what you all have to say for yourselves."

The circle of women exchanged various looks without response. Finally, the real estate lady, Robin, said, "What do you expect us to say?" She had her handbag in her lap, clutching it with both hands.

"I just think you should all be ashamed of yourselves," Sissy said. "He's my husband. And, if you have an ounce of decency, you will admit to your indiscretions and agree to stop seeing him."

"Es'cuse me!" Rosario said. She'd been sitting with her legs crossed, picking at long nails. Now she sat forward, her short skirt riding up. "Indiscretions? No! I don't think so! If he was getting it good at home he would not be coming to Rosario each night, would he."

"And if you're such a hot number, sweetie, how come he leaves your bed to come to me?" Eleanor said, her voice dripping molasses. She tossed her head in a sophisticated manner, the diamonds at her earlobes jiggled.

"Girl's got a point," Babe said.

"You better believe it," someone said beneath their breath.

"I don't see it!" Rosario scoffed. She fell back into her seat, crossing her legs once more, and turned away to pout.

Robin said to the group, "Is it just me or is Sissy bein' rude? I mean, you don't just invite a person to your home and start criticizing them."

"He's my husband," Sissy said. She was wringing her hands hard enough that red blotches were beginning to appear. "You're all so callous, I don't see how Billy could have been with any of you."

"It is simple, darling." This time it was Helga, speaking in a husky Slavic accent. She put a cigarette to her lips and lit it. "He is a man."

"How can you be so nonchalant about it, Helga? I happen to know you've outwardly stalked my husband."

Helga drew on her cigarette coolly. "Helga stalks no one. He is a big boy, is he not?"

"This was not the way it was supposed to happen!" Sissy said, rising quickly from her chair. "My therapist, Doctor Lauren, said I should confront you. Each of you, she said, and seek assurances you will end these affairs. But this is turning into a nightmare. You're not remorseful! Any of you! And I've heard no one offer to end the affair!" Sissy stood rigid before them, defiant, chin jutting, her fists clinched at her sides.

There was no response from the group, only solemn stares. Slowly Sissy deflated. She sank to her seat, wiping at the tears that had welled in her eyes. Speaking more to herself, than to the others, she said, "Doctor Lauren said it was the only way to get better."

The bulk of the group sat quietly, eyes downcast, with nothing else to add. All except Marta, who continued to observe them closely. At last she grew weary. "Oh, for Chistsakes! This is too much! First of all, listen to yourself, Sissy. Whine, whine, whine...You think you're so special? Well think again. You're not the only victim here. And the rest of you," she said, turning on the others. "What the hell have you got to hang your heads about?"

Marta rose now and came around to position herself behind her chair. Using it like a podium to address the group, she said, "It seems to me we're all victims of Billy Tingle's chauvinistic rituals. He's obviously been using each of us in some kind of sick, rotational free-for-all. Look around! We're like a circus menagerie. A Realtor, a construction worker. How about a hot-blooded salsa queen?"

"You'd better believe it, sister," Rosario chimed in.

"We're as different as night and day," Marta continued. "Eleanor, our debutant from Houston. Does he make you talk dirty to him, sweetheart? And Helga. What are you, some kind of anarchist? Maybe you think of yourself as a vamp. Have you ever actually made love to Billy Tingle, or do you only allow him to watch while you pleasure yourself?"

Helga shrugged indifferently and blew a cloud of smoke at the chandelier.

"There's no need for hostilities, I'm sure," Robin said.

"Yeah, watch yourself, Marta," Babe added. "You're in this too."

"Look, I don't mean to offend any of you," Marta said. "I'm simply calling attention to the fact that our Billy Tingle seems to have a taste for variety. It causes me to wonder who'll be next. A female rock star? A preacher's daughter? If we held this meeting three months from now would there be ten chairs instead of seven? Twenty?"

"Are you saying we should all break up with him?" Robin asked.

"Such a simpleton," Helga said. She stubbed her cigarette and reached for another to light. "Marta is leading up to something, can't you see that?"

"Is that right? If you've got something to say, Marta, maybe you should spit it out," Babe said.

Marta took in the circle with her eyes.

"I'm just saying that we've all been duped. Okay, he's Sissy's husband. But Billy Tingle is the villain, here, not us. And I'm betting that if we compared notes we'd find out just how often we've been lied to and cheated on."

"I'm sure I don't know what y'all are talking about," Eleanor said, toying with an earring. "Billy was always honest with me. In fact, regardless of whatever past he's had with each of you, it's over now. Billy has asked me to marry him just as soon as he can divorce his little wallflower of a wife."

"Es'cuse me! But you don't know nothing you're saying. Billy promised to marry me."

"Well you can join the club," Babe said. "Billy proposed to me from the back of my scooter."

"How romantic," Helga added.

"Regardless, you've made my point exactly," Marta said. "What about the rest of you? Billy make you any promises he couldn't keep?"

Helga raised her hand in a bored way. "He said he was taking me to Paris."

Eleanor said. "He was taking me to see the pyramids, but I sure can't say I've seen the airline tickets."

"And he planned to buy me my own customized chopper," Babe said.

"Well, he never promised me no such things, I can tell you that," Rosario said. "He just do coochie-coochie-coochie all the time. Not one word about buying me something nice."

"That has got to piss you off," Eleanor said.

"Like I want to cut his tiny manhood off and feed it to the chupa cabre," Rosario said.

Sissy stomped her foot. "I don't believe any of you!"

"Well, you'd better believe it, little sister," Marta said. "Billy Tingle has been having his way with all of us. And I for one am not liking it one bit."

Marta came around to take her seat. She leaned into the circle, drawing the others into her confidence. "How long are we prepared, ladies, to let ourselves be used?"

"I don't know about the rest of you," Babe said. "But I've had my share of backdoor men in my life. I say, whatever we do, it includes making that little weasel pay."

"I agree," Robin said.

"Likewise," Eleanor added. "But that begs the question…What exactly do we do?"

Marta deferred to the group. "I'm open to suggestions."

"We could publicly humiliate him," Robin offered. "Cause trouble with his employer."

"Humiliate him?" Babe said. "Honey, the more I listen, the more I hear. All those times he told me he was too busy to see me? He was too busy all right. Busy boffin' all of you. Just thinking about it makes me want to have his legs broken. And I know a couple of bikers who'd do it for the price of a beer."

"Now we're getting to the point," Marta said. "Keep going."

"Es'cuse me!" Rosario said. "But, break his legs…No good! What happens when he gets the cast off?"

"In my country," Helga said, "they cut out your tongue for lying, cut off your hands for putting them where they don't belong. Maybe this man should be castrated."

"Stop it!" Sissy cried. "You're sick! All of you! You need help!" She grappled for control of her emotions. "Please…" she said, pleading now, trying to reason with the others. "If Doctor Lauren were here, she would tell you you're all just acting-out. If we would only take time to explore our feelings, I know we can…"

"Put a lid on it, sister," Babe said.

"Yeah! Cut the psychobabble, Sissy. This isn't about you anymore," Robin added.

"I've heard some very good ideas," Marta said. "But I, for one, am sick and tired of men and their lying, cheating ways. Leaving them is too good for them. Causing them financial ruin isn't permanent enough. And beating the hell out of them is like eating Chinese food. An hour later you want to do it again."

Heads nodded agreement about the circle.

"You've got something in mind, Marta," Babe said. Why don't you tell us what it is."

"I'm thinking we make it so that double-crossing little worm can't do to other women what he's been doing to us."

"Here! Here!" Robin said.

"He deserves the worst," Helga said coolly.

"I say ditto to that, what you said," Rosario agreed.

"All right then, I think its time we take a vote," Marta said, coming to her feet. "All in favor of killing Billy Tingle…raise your hand."

Babe's hand shot up first, followed by Robin's. Helga raised hers in a slow unhurried way. "Le's do it," Rosario said, lifting her palm. Eleanor showed them a gloved hand, "What the hell? It looks like my trip to the pyramids is out anyway."

All faces turned to Sissy, now, who sat, eyes in her lap, wringing her hands. Finally she looked up. "I can't believe what I'm hearing. Billy is a good man. Even after all this, he doesn't deserve to die. I cannot be a part of this, I'm sorry. I'm calling Doctor Lauren, right now."

Sissy rose and quickly left the room.

Robin called after her. "Sissy…!"

"Let her go," Helga said. "We don't need her."

"Helga's right," Babe said. "By the time the good Doc drives out from the city that little weasel, Billy, will be history. And we'll all be long gone."

"All right," Marta said. "Any ideas how we do it?"

Helga reached deep inside her boot and pulled a small Derringer. Dangling the cigarette from the corner of her mouth and squinting back the smoke, she expertly broke it down and checked the load. Satisfied, she slapped it shut and displayed it to the others. "The question is who gets the pleasure of pulling the trigger."

"Give it to me…" Rosario said, waving the gun over. "What did this *wetto* ever do for me, anyway, besides add circles under my eyes?"

Helga passed the gun around the circle to Rosario—each woman taking time to admire and caress the cold chrome before handing it on.

When the gun was securely in Rosario's grip, Marta said. "Approximately twenty minutes. I guess all we have to do now is wait for Billy."

The doorbell rang at a quarter past ten.

In the parlor, Sissy sat alone, the spent Derringer lying on the chair next to her. Her gaze was held on the body near the door—Billy Tingle lying in a pool of his own blood. He was a small, balding man, in an ill-fitting business suit. His features in death were, as they had been in life, unbalanced and unattractive.

Again, the doorbell rang.

Sissy, keeping her gaze on the body, called through the doorway. "Come in."

Doctor Jane Lauren entered the parlor. An attractive woman, in her late thirties, she was dressed in a modest dark skirt, a pale blue blouse. Her hair was drawn back in a simple matching ribbon. At her feet, blood ran a tributary from Billy to the hallway.

"What have you done, Sissy?" Doctor Lauren said, maintaining her calm.

Sissy continued to stare at the body.

Doctor Lauren sat her briefcase on floor and entered the circle to stand over Sissy.

"Is this your husband, Sissy? Is this Billy?"

Sissy nodded, not looking up.

"Have the police been notified?"

"They're on their way," Sissy said softly.

"Did you do this? Did you kill Billy?"

"It wasn't me. It was the others."

"The others?"

Sissy nodded again. "Marta, Babe, Helga, Eleanor, Robin, and the other one, the Hispanic woman, Rosario. They wanted me to help them." Sissy looked up now, her eyes red and wet with tears. "But I couldn't do it. I loved Billy. I did."

Beyond the drawn curtains, the sound of police sirens could be heard approaching fast. In the parlor, Sissy sat wringing her hands, Doctor Lauren studying her.

"Sissy, you're going to have to go with the police when they arrive, you know that don't you?"

Sissy nodded.

"Do you understand why?"

"What we talked about?" Sissy said quietly.

"Yes," Doctor Lauren said. "Do you remember? Marta and the others aren't real. They're part of you. It's called Multiple Personality Syndrome. Do you recall we talked about it?"

Sissy looked up now. "I think it was Rosario that shot him."

"I'm sure it was," Doctor Lauren said. "And I'll be right beside you when you tell the police. Okay?"

"Okay," Sissy said.

Doctor Lauren took Sissy by the elbow and lifted her from the chair. She led her that way, out the door, gathering her briefcase as they went.

At the door, Sissy paused. She turned her eyes back to the body on the floor. "Do I have to mention that Billy was sleeping with all those other women?" She looked to Doctor Lauren. "It's kind of embarrassing."

Doctor Lauren studied Sissy's face, the innocence residing there. "Only if you want to, Sissy," she said. "Only if you want to."

SOMETHING HEAVY
WHEN YOU NEED IT

Again, tonight, he was drinking and having his way with her—his weight upon her from the back, a wad of her freshly brushed hair bunched in his fist, her face pushed into the bedding. There was a familiar sour odor beneath her in the fabric—previous encounters—and his enraged animal sounds above. He plunged at her the way one might attempt to clear a stubborn drain. It made her think of the chores she'd left undone.

Beyond the bed, at eye-level, the alarm clock marked time. She watched the second hand sweep its way around the dial. *It's the minutes and hours that take so long.* She wondered if he would finish fast tonight, and if sleep would overtake him afterwards as it sometimes did. And she wondered what other young girls were doing with their fathers this night...

Calliopes play. Lights glitter. Colorfully painted ponies—up-then-down—chase each other 'round and 'round. His hand is big and strong, hers is small and frail. Entwined. There is laughter and noise and dazzling motion. The promise of untold mysteries revealed in the carneys' calls. Ten going on eleven. An alien stir of sexuality. Strange. Unsettling.

Clickity-clickity-clickity.

Cars and humanity tilt on the edge of the world. Screams. Laughter. Off into nothing. Cotton candy sticks to her nose. Her tongue fishes it away. Remember it all, she thinks, every last moment.

They ride a washy-wave through a clown's mouth. Boat beneath, Daddy beside. Happy music leads the way into darkness and then fades beneath the drowning weight of a dirge. Anxious. Delicious. Wonderful dread. A ghost here? Maybe. A turn there? No. A flash of pitch-forked devil. The boat knocks against concrete; concrete knocks against boat. She feels her father's hand on her knee. Reassurance, she thinks. Safe, she feels.

Sounds. Sights. Colors. A gargoyle's laughter. But darkness, mostly darkness.

Off, but clear. Approaching. A train's whistle. A round spot of light in the blackness. It sheds its clear, white purity on them. Daddy's hand high beneath her skirt. A mother's warning—what was it?—something puzzling. Something worrisome. Where was Mommy now? Gone away. The cancer.

The whistle blows; the headlight grows. Fingers touch at hidden flesh. Daddy...? His face is fixed on the distance. Warning. The whistle grows.

The spot of light swells. A cast iron thudding in her chest. Heavy metal grinding near. The sound. *Shooka-shooka-shooka.* It can't be shaken. The light. Bright. It can't be dimmed. Is there nothing to put out that awful eye? Something heavy, she considers, something swung with all ones might...Now!

Doors bang open. The carney's voice. Cars on the edge of the world. Laughter. Screams. The boat bumps to a docky end. His hand touches her no more. But something wet remains. Ugliness. Not of your doing, she tells herself. Remember nothing. Nothing of this night...

It lasted longer than usual this time, and sleep, the blessed savior, did not hit him. Instead, he made his way out and down the hall, television sounds coming at the end of his footsteps. Lura cleaned herself at the basin, touching at the purple and yellow bruises between her thighs. Some were old and dying, others were galactic nebulas, still forming. She wondered if other girls were made to nurse themselves in this manner. It was a worn thought, dredged up for reassessment. She finished quickly and hurried down the hall where Father would be waiting.

She found him in the recliner, the remote in one hand—his usual place, when he wasn't knocking at her door. She came to stand behind him. "You going to want dinner tonight?" she asked.

His only reply was a grunt of sorts. His only look came from the single bald spot at the back of his head.

Was it so easy for him to rationalize, she wondered? Or did he work to cover his shame? Co-mingled with normal fathers—fathers who weren't having sex with their daughters—did he blend? Or did others—say, passers on the street—read some *tell* in his gaze?

The bald spot seemed to be watching her—this evil eye. A bright, white spot amid surrounding blackness. It stared at her across the back of the leather recliner, looming large, bearing down on her. Somewhere off and from another time a train whistle warned. Lura shook the one-eyed gaze.

"I'll have to microwave something," she said, "I'm still fixin' on the sink."

"Bring me a beer while you're at it," her father said—said it without looking at her and without shifting that hideous bald eye. Lura broke its gaze and went off to comply.

In the kitchen, Lura took time to survey the mess she'd left behind. The under-sink cabinet doors stood ajar. The gooseneck pipes and fittings lay disassembled. A pan beneath the open drain stood filled with brown water and sludge. There were tools strewn about. And the wooden box she'd hauled them up from the basement in.

A heavy, cast iron pipe wrench, used to break-loose the fittings, lay discarded on the tile. All were mid-job-abandoned when he'd called her to his bed. Him— the one who'd admonished her to *fix the damn leak*.

Cinderella, she thought to say. But the wicked stepsisters didn't hold Cinderella down and make her do things, did they. They didn't invite themselves upon her the way her father did.

Lura crossed to the refrigerator and opened the door...

Brown beer bottles stand lined in formation. She takes one in her hand, removes it from the rest. Behind, light from the bare refrigerator bulb breaks though. A spot that reaches her from between the milk carton, the leftover Chinese, the bottles. And darkness. Mostly darkness. Off in the distance, a train's whistle blows. Speeding, it finds urgency and cries. Heavy metal reverberates inside her chest. *Shooka-shooka-shooka*. The sound fills her ears. Fingers probe soft flesh. Mother's voice warns.

The white spot of light in the distance expands, grows nearer. Painful bright. Is there nothing with which to put out that one awful eye? Something heavy—a thing remembered—something swung with all ones might.

Lura raises the beer bottle in her hand. No, she has abandoned that chore, she realizes. The thing—this thing—in her hand is more sufficient. Something heavy when you need it. She looks at it, raised high: the pipe wrench from the kitchen floor. Something to put out that one damned eye...

Lura took one last look at the bald spot at the back of her father's head, then brought the wrench down with force. The sound it made was simple—a *pump-*

kin-thump sound—and her father went slack in his chair. With an odd detachment, Lura looked at the bloody pipe wrench in her hand. *Where were you when I needed you?* she thought. Then wondered if she was speaking of the wrench or of her mother who had died too soon. Oh, well, she thought, there was still dinner to serve, and, of course, there were still pipes beneath the drain that needed refitting. One thing, for sure, she considered…she would never have to look into that terrible light ever again.

KAT & MOUSE

Monday, Detectives Frank Delgado and Julius Lemon weren't sure if they were dealing with a homicide or not. The call had come from a Professor Madeline Wainright, an Administrator at the University Anatomy Department at UCLA. Something troubling about her cadaver count, she'd said on the phone. The two detectives agreed they didn't know you had to *bed check* your cadavers but accepted that maybe it was an okay idea in case one or more of them decided to walk off.

What they found when they showed up at the lab was a dozen or more torsos on surgical work tables that weren't going anywhere. Most were missing limbs; some were missing heads; others had gaping holes in their chests where vital organs had been removed. The parts, along with the severed heads lay or sat in stainless steel surgical trays nearby.

"We don't do gross anatomy procedures these days, Detectives," Professor Wainright explained, seeing the question in their eyes. She was an aging prune who looked only one step away from one of the surgical trays herself. "It's a practical matter. One team can be working on dissecting a brain or a limb, while others might be exploring the thoracic regions of the chest or the vascular complexities of the heart."

"Uh-huh," Delgado said, not knowing what else to say. Julius simply stood with his eyes fixed on the severed heads.

"I assure you," she continued, "we take our work seriously, Detective. Every donated cadaver is carefully separated and all the parts are identified with a unique numbering system. They're accounted for at the beginning and end of each school week. We won't tolerate tomfoolery. We're constantly looking for shortages to tell us if someone is stealing our parts. College students can be pranksters, you know."

"Pranksters," Delgado said. He turned to Julius, wanting his reaction, but found him poking one of the torsos with a pointed tool as if expecting it to giggle.

"Stop that, please!" Wainright said, locking Julius in her gaze.

Julius laid the tool aside and shoved his hands inside his pockets to keep them out of trouble.

Wainright held him with her eyes a moment longer before releasing him, then said, "The problem, you see, is this..."

She led them across the lab to stop before one of the severed heads, that of an elderly Asian man.

What struck Delgado was the wide grin strapped across the man's face—in death and dismemberment, the man still seemingly happy.

"Kamikaze Bob?" Delgado said, reading from the name tag taped to the table just below the head.

"Yes. The students sometimes name their cadavers. A silly but harmless ritual. They have to work hard, as you might imagine, to objectify the real person represented by the body parts on the table. You deal with bodies in your line of work also, Detective. Perhaps you can understand?"

He could.

Delgado said, "Okay, so you're telling us Bob's got some body parts missing. Why exactly did you call homicide?"

Wainright gave them both a look of incredulity. "I'm not saying Kamikaze Bob represents shortages, Detectives...I'm saying he's extra."

On the CHS Plaza outside the School of Medicine, Frank Delgado and Julius Lemon stood watching Med Students making their way between classes. Across Charles E. Young Drive, where the main part of campus resided, the buildings were old and stately. Here they had the starch of newness about them.

Delgado looked out beyond campus toward the city and felt a sadness he hadn't seen coming.

"You ever wish you could go back and do it all over again," Delgado said. "Imagine spending your youth at an institution like this?"

"Yeah, and all the young 'tang around here, you'd be flunked out first semester and still wind up walking a beat. So what?"

"What do you think about Miss Wainright?"

Julius said, "Aside from being old as rock, I think she's telling us Kamikaze Bob doesn't belong here."

"And she has a good argument," Delgado said. "The numbered tag on Bob doesn't match their records. So I guess the question is, 'Who is Bob?' and 'How he'd get here?'"

"What I want to know, personally," Julius said. "How come the dude's grinning like that? Man was freaking me out."

Delgado withdrew a piece of paper from his coat pocket. "I guess there's only one way to find out...ask these two. 'Katherine Dunbar and Moselle Williams.' The students have magnetic pass cards that let them in and out of the lab. The security system says they were the only ones logged in after the last cadaver count on Friday. I'll have a black and white pick them up."

"Katherine and Moselle, huh," Julius said. "Sound like someone's grandmas to me."

The next day, Tuesday, a black and white brought them in, and the girls were anything but grandmas.

"My God, would you look at them," Julius Lemon said. "Man, they are fucking beautiful."

They were. Beyond the one-way glass, at either end of a metal table, looking bored.

The tall and buxom blonde with her legs crossed, wore what could only be thought of as a Catholic schoolgirl uniform—blouse unbuttoned to reveal the bra line, an ultra short pleated skirt and Bobby socks. Her girlfriend, a five-foot tall, African-American mocha cappuccino, wore skin-tight blue jeans and a silk scarf tied across her breasts. From where the Detectives stood, peering through the glass, they saw lots of bare skin.

"So what do you think?" Delgado said. "Think these two are capable of foul play?"

Julius, Delgado knew, was a pretty good gauge of character, particularly when it came to women. He was stylish and trim, turning thirty-four the end of the month. And not bad looking for a black guy, Delgado guessed, though he was no Denzel Washington.

Julius said, "Ain't nothing foul 'bout these two. But just me, mind you, I've seen people do things for love or money you'd never suspect."

"Well, I guess there's only one way to find out? Let's go grill these heartbreakers."

The girls looked up as Delgado and Julius entered the interview room. The little one sat forward, while the tall blonde slumped further in her seat, crossing her arms across her breasts, and flashing a hint of white panty at her crotch.

Delgado felt suddenly old. He was coming up on his fifty-second birthday, and he hadn't been able to see his feet without leaning forward in almost ten years. He sucked-in his stomach and ran fingers through his thinning hair in a nervous gesture. Catching Julius staring at the blonde's legs beneath her short skirt, he turned his own gaze toward the little mocha girl. She had the most flawless skin he'd ever seen.

"I'm Detective Frank Delgado," he said, clearing his throat, "and this is my partner, Detective Julius Lemon."

The small girl folded her hands primly in her lap; the blonde looked off with a bored expression.

"Which one of you is Katherine?"

The blonde raised her hand without looking at him, not putting much into it. "I'm Katherine, she's Moselle."

Julius said, "You ladies are med students at UCLA, we understand."

"Pre-med," Katherine corrected.

"Pre-Med, uh-huh, that's cool. So tell me, what do you do with your free time?"

"You asking us out?"

Delgado stepped in. "My partner's just trying to ascertain the manner in which you make your living."

Listen to yourself, he thought, *ascertain the manner in which you make your living*—Jesus!—what the hell was wrong with him? He said, "Do you have jobs?"

"We're entertainers, part time," Moselle said, keeping her eyes buried in her hands.

Julius said, "Entertainers, huh."

Mouse reached into her back pocket and withdrew a business card. She handed it to him.

Julius looked the card over, grinning, then handed it to Delgado.

Delgado read aloud, "KAT & MOUSE—Bachelor Parties, Special Occasions, Private Sessions. I see you have a 24 hour pager. You must be very popular."

He stuffed the card into his shirt pocket, then said, "Tell me...what kind of entertainment, exactly, would this be?"

Mouse offered, "We dance."

"And you take your clothes off," Julius said.

"We strip, yes, and dance. Sometimes we let the customer take pictures."

"And then you get friendly with him or them," Julius said.

"Sometimes the two of us fool around with each other a little bit. It's all for show. I guess there's something about two girls making it together that turns a lot of guys on."

"Then you all kind of get in a big pile, maybe."

"Oh for Christsake!" Kat said. "You want to know if we turn tricks? Well the answer is no! Never! We have a rule about direct contact. But beyond that we try to give our clients what they want. Christ! Do you have any idea how much Med School costs?"

"Pre-med," Delgado said.

"What?"

"You said you were Pre-med."

"Whatever," Kat said, turning away again.

Delgado looked the two girls over. He pictured a bachelor party, a dozen guys ganged around with plastic cups full of beer. Or maybe a private show in a hotel room, a couple of businessmen from out of town. He let the image of the two young women making love to one another enter his mind. The contrast between them was striking. And erotic—Christ!—so goddamn erotic. "Do you know why you're here?" he said.

Kat said, "Something about one too many cadavers at the Anatomy Lab. I don't see what that's got to do with us."

"Nothing," Delgado said, "unless you can tell us how an extra one got there."

Kat turned away again.

Delgado looked to Mouse. "What about you? There anything you can tell us?"

Mouse lowered her eyes.

Julius said, "Looky here, ladies! We can do this the hard way, you want. We can get a warrant, look for the man's DNA on your G-strings, your sequined bras. We'll take it before a Grand Jury, see what they have to say."

"Good luck," Kat said, beneath her breath.

"What?"

Kat straightened in her seat, not bothering to lower the hem of her skirt. "Look, you can do all the forensic testing you want. What you'll find is this cadaver's DNA everywhere! On our shoes, on our clothes, on clothes in contact with clothes in our laundry basket, dragged home from the lab where we worked on every piece of the body. Then while you're at it, you can check the homes of the half-dozen other students who worked on it with us, as members of our Dissection Team, first period lab. Check their homes, their shoes, their clothes, their laundry baskets. Then what have you've got?"

The girl was smart, Delgado had to admit. The body's DNA had been scattered everywhere. Mixed with other DNA: moved, transferred, mingled some more. There was no identifiable crime scene to rope off, or for that matter an identifiable crime. Still, something about these two…He said, "Do you ever entertain clients at your apartment?"

The question seemed to stall them. It was almost imperceptible, but a quick glance passed between them. The blonde stiffened

"Sometimes," Kat said.

"Let's just say, hypothetically and off the record, we did wipe your place down…You think we'd find traces of certain body fluids, let's say such things as semen that might be hard to explain from just laboratory contact with the cadaver?"

It was a long shot, Delgado knew, a bluff. Even if they tossed the girls apartment, the chances of them finding anything that would stand up in a courtroom was slim. But he did have the blonde's attention, now, he could tell.

"Hypothetically?" Kat said.

"You're not under oath here. We haven't read you your rights. We're just a couple of working guys looking to complete a call report, you understand."

Kat looked to Mouse. Delgado watched silent communications running between the two girls. Finally Kat said, "There might be a way it could happen."

"If there is I'd like to hear it," Delgado said.

"Can I get a cigarette first?"

Delgado looked to Julius who came out with a pack. He offered it to Kat, who took one and waited with it poised while he offered one to Mouse. The smaller girl declined, and now Julius lit Kat's cigarette for her and stepped back.

Kat drew smoke into her lungs and exhaled slowly. "So, now where were we?"

"You were about to tell us a story," Delgado said.

"Yeah, right, so let's see. Once upon a time…"

Friday nights were reserved for Mr. Nguyen.

The little Asian man would sit in a straight-back chair in the center of the room and chirp directions in Vietnamese, while his wife, watching from the sofa, would translate.

"He say, 'Take time! Go slow!'"

The girls, Kat and Mouse, didn't understand a word Mr. Nguyen said but would take the wife's directions and ease into a slow fluid groove, taking their time with buttons and hooks, removing articles of clothing in slow teasing strokes.

Sometimes—Fridays when Mister Nguyen was feeling particularly spunky—he'd ask them to get it on together. Why not? They would swap a little spit, twirl their tongues inside each other's mouth and pretend they were turning each other on. They could moan and put on dreamy, faraway expressions, and slide their hands over each other's bodies, until Mister Nguyen spotted the front of his trousers. They could do all this and not feel dirty. It paid the rent.

"So how is Mr. Nguyen tonight?" Kat asked, leading the little Vietnamese man to his usual seat in the hardback chair.

Kat on these occasions was known as Blondie. As in: "He say, tell Blondie bend over, spread. Moselle would then become the Little One, or the Black Girl. "He say, have little one touch self. Tell black girl turn around."

Mrs. Nguyen said, "You watch self, Blondie. He try put in me. I tell him, 'No way Joe.'" She took her seat on the sofa and pulled out an open pack of cigarettes from her bag.

The evening began as usual, the girls getting into the mood, lighting incense and getting into a slow steady sway to the sounds of Barry White. Mrs. Nguyen sat watching from the sofa, chain smoking cigarettes in a bored way. Mr. Nguyen, his eyes glued on one or the other of them, would occasionally lick the dryness from his lips, then shift his gaze to the other.

"He say, little girl take off pants," Mrs. Nguyen said.

They were down to their g-strings and kissing by the time the Barry White album ended and the CD changer made a switch to Billy Holliday. Mrs. Nguyen finished off her partial pack of cigarettes and opened a fresh one. There was a rise in the little man's pants. Now and then he would come off his chair and grab for one of them, and Kat, being the big girl in the room, would have to put him down.

They continued their routine, watching for that time when Mr. Nguyen would buck back stiff in his chair, signaling an end to the night's entertainment. They were waiting for it when Mrs. Nguyen said. "How you girls like to make extra tonight?"

"Extra?" Kat said, continuing to dance. "We don't turn tricks. I thought you understood that."

"You smart girls. Not tricks."

"Then what," Mouse said.

"You tie up," Mrs. Nguyen said.

Kat stopped dancing. "Excuse me?"

"You tie, he like."

"Did he tell you that?" Kat asked. She hadn't heard Mr. Nguyen say anything, the man grinning and staring at her crotch.

"He tell me earlier," Mrs. Nguyen said, "Also say, he want flog with pillows."

Kat looked to Mouse.

Mouse shrugged. "Man wants to be flogged, what's the harm. We could use the money."

They bound the old man's wrists to the arms of the chair with the sequined bras that had previously been discarded. Mouse gathered throw pillows from the sofa.

The look on Mr. Nguyen's face was hard to read. He'd become quiet, as they cinched his bindings tight. At one point he winced, but grinned harder. And there was no mistaking the huge tent in the little man's pants.

Mouse gave Kat a brief glance, then cocked the pillow high overhead.

"Wait!" Katherine said.

She handed Mouse her pillow to hold, then moved to the CD player and switched the music. When Nirvana came on with a blast, she returned and took the pillow.

"If you're going to do it, do it right," she said.

To Heavy Metal drive the girls began to slap Mr. Nguyen with the throw pillows—easy at first and then, gauging the excitement in the old man's voice, harder.

Mrs. Nguyen came alive for the first time, sitting forward and stubbing out her cigarette, she issued instructions.

"He say harder!" She shouted above the blast of music.

Naked to their g-strings the girls increased their aggression. Sweat glistened on their skin and across the old man's brow.

"He say, harder! Harder!" Mrs. Nguyen cried.

"You sure this is what Mr. Nguyen wants?" Kat said.

"Say, make hurt!" Mrs. Nguyen said.

Mr. Nguyen's grin remained wide as the girls increased their aggression, but now it had a kind of sickly sag to it. He was straining against his bonds, sinews twanged in his neck.

"You think he can take this," Mouse said to Kat, slamming the pillow down hard across Mr. Nguyen's neck and shoulder. "I can't tell if he's having an orgasm or a heart attack."

"I think that's enough," Kat said, lowering her pillow and stepping back. She crossed to the CD player and killed the music.

Mouse ceased swinging also.

"Okay," Mrs. Nguyen said, "I pay now." She came off the sofa to toss a wad of bills on the table. She gathered her bag and stowed her cigarettes

"I think you should take a look at Mr. Nguyen," Kat said.

"He fine," Mrs. Nguyen said. Now she was heading toward the door.

"Wait, where are you going? What about Mr. Nguyen?"

"Have to go bye-bye now. You finish!" she said, and was out the door...

"She just leaves," Delgado said.

"Walks out and leaves the girls cold," Kat said, leaning across the table to stub her cigarette in the ashtray.

"What about the old man? Julius said. He'd been leaning against the wall with his arms crossed. "Don't forget we got a head on a tray at the lab."

Kat and Mouse shared a look.

Kat said, "It's a story with multiple possible endings. Call it Director's Cuts."

"Let me see if I can fill it in," Delgado said. "In one scenario the old man croaks of a heart attack with a wet spot on his pants—an accident. In another, the old guy's doing just fine, grinning from ear to ear, but the girls, at the old woman's bequest, simply finish the job." Delgado leveled his eyes on Kat. "Which one should we believe?"

Kat shrugged.

Delgado turned to Mouse, "You got anything to add to this?"

"She's telling it," Mouse said. "Me and her are partners."

Delgado said, "Un-huh."

Julius stepped off the wall. "You ladies will excuse us for a second." He motioned Delgado to the door.

In the hall and alone now, Delgado said to Julius.

"You understand where this is leading?"

"I understand why the old man's still grinning," Julius said.

"There girls are telling us they were involved, but what have we really got? We've got forensics that have been highly compromised and a ridiculous story that could always be recanted under oath. That's it."

Julius shook his head. "Jesus, would you look at them in there? You ever seen girls so beautiful."

"And smart too," Delgado said. "Kat, the tall, cool one. She knows exactly where they stand."

The men stood watching the girls through the glass for a time, then without further comment went back inside.

"You're free to go," Delgado told the girls. "But there is one thing I don't understand. In your hypothetical story, why did *the girls* take the body to the anatomy lab? Why not bury it or dump it in the L.A. River or something?"

Mouse said, more as a question than a statement of fact, "Donate the body to science?"

Delgado turned to Kat. "That your answer?"

"To further the cause of medicine?"

They were smart girls. "Go on, get out of here," he said.

The two men watched them go.

With the girls gone, all that was left was a heavy longing. Julius said, "Man, leaves you drained doesn't it?"

"Yes, it does," Delgado said.

"So, what do we tell the old bag at the University?"

"We tell her to recheck her cadaver count. I'm sure she's mistaken." He retrieved the girls' business card from his shirt pocket. "KAT & MOUSE," he said, and tossed the card into the nearby wastebasket. "Come on, I'll buy you a beer."

Delgado headed off but turned at the door to find Julius fishing through the wastebasket. He watched as Julius came out with the card, watched him stand and look it over. When Julius turned toward the door, only then, did they make eye contact.

"What?" Julius said.

"You understand," Delgado said, "there's a fifty-fifty chance these girls actually killed the guy for money. Made the choice and did it. You want your head to wind up on a baking sheet?"

Julius said, "Did you see the smile on the dude's face?"

"Yeah," Delgado said, picturing the silly, relentless grin on Kamikaze Bob. "You're right. It may just be worth it."

THE BRIDGE

It straddled the ravine on tall, concrete columns: one lane of asphalt-covered timbers, sixty feet above the railroad tracks. More rough-hewn timbers clutched at the base of the columns and held hands in crisscrossed patterns to support the center span. It was the only way into and out of the small town, where, along Division Street, storefronts huddled at a safe distance and watched the old structure with a wary eye. At least, that's the way it seemed to Robert Anderson.

Robert stood in the center of the street and studied the bridge. It had been thirty years since he'd last seen the wretched thing, but the memory of the rotting timbers had continued to visit him each night in dreams throughout his life. The doctors had called them *Night Terrors*.

The *terrors* had started the summer of sixty-one, the year he'd reached his seventeenth birthday. The same year the town witnessed the most vicious and brutal crime of its history: the bloody slaying of five teenagers—their bodies found slashed and mutilated beneath the bridge, parts tossed and scattered along the tracks, their blood soaked into the wooden timbers. The teens had been Robert's classmates. More importantly, one had been *Jenny*—the love of his life Jenny—and the bridge, that damned evil thing, had become the focus of his terror. There had been six months spent in feverish delirium, followed by the dreams that were so devastating that his parents were forced to flee with him to a small town in Arizona, far from the horror of those events.

The bridge was older now, of course, and crumbling. No longer in use, wooden barriers barred access to it. Signs read: "Danger—Weak Timbers" and "Keep Out." It would be easy to turn around and go back, Robert considered, leave the damned thing to cave in atop itself. But he had come to face it, to seek a possible end to the tormenting nightmares. And it had, after all, taken him so long to find the courage.

With leaden feet, Robert crossed to where the barriers stood. Brittle wooden slats gave way to his touch and he stepped over and onto the broken asphalt surface. He tested his weight before going farther.

At the center of the bridge, he stopped and peered across the railing. Sunlight glinted off the shiny rails below. The ravine wasn't as deep as he remembered or imagined in his dreams, still, a light dizziness fell over him.

"Don't go near the bridge."

It was his mother's voice he heard. His mother, dead more than seven years now—still he could hear her words in the still, stale air. *"Don't go near the bridge, Bobby."* Despite the warning, Robert reached a trembling hand to the bridge's railing.

Nothing happened at first, and Robert considered leaving. What had he expected, after all? But then a trembling began beneath his touch, grew stronger, and a sudden brilliant flash of light struck him. Behind it came darkness.

...seventeen-year-old *Bobby* Anderson sat crouched inside the narrow alleyway that separated Brewers' grocery from Nordman's Stag Bar. His stripped down Huffy bicycle sat next to him, leaned against the shingled siding of the building. The night was cool, and the darkness unnerved him, but it was a good spot from which to view the bridge.

Over there, where light from the storefronts cast their glow, they sat gathered like crows along the bridge's railing: classmates of Bobby's, all of them. There was Cecil Johnson, the *weasel*, with his orange-red hair and Howdy Doodie freckles. There was Buddy Seitz, the *slob*, his t-shirt hanging half-in, half-out of his pants. And there was Kevin Curry. Bobby tried to think of a name for Kevin but couldn't come up with anything fitting. He was the popular one, at least by standard opinion: tight jeans, a black leather jacket over his white T-shirt: *Mister Quarterback, Mister All-Conference, Mister "Oh-So Cool."* The three passed around a quart bottle of Hudepohl and drank from it. Their voices were loud.

"Don't go near the bridge, Bobby."

He didn't want to be here. The place scared him a little. And it was these kids, Kevin and the others, his mother had warned about. But he had to find out, once and for all, if *Jenny Conner* would show.

"She was there last week, I saw her," Jason Raymond, *Jay-Ray*, had told him earlier in the day during lunch break.

"Did not. She wouldn't! She likes me."

"Ask Donnie, you don't believe me. He says she goes there all the time."

Jay-Ray was lying, Bobby believed, was sure of it. And he'd prove it if he had to sit here all night. Honest to God, all week.

Jenny was *his* girl.

He thought of Jenny now, how beautiful she was. He liked the way her long hair danced at the small of her back when she walked, or when she did cheers for the football team. He liked the way she smelled. Always something of lilac on her delicate skin. And he liked the way she touched; tender, sincere. He could feel her fingertips now the way he'd felt them after school earlier that day when he'd asked her to go out with him. She hadn't said yes. And she hadn't said no. But she had laid her fingers on his cheek with that soft, delicate touch.

"You're a nice guy, Bobby."

She had told him that. Wasn't that a sign? Wasn't that like saying she liked him, really liked him, a lot? And Kevin Curry, Mister Cool, she could never, ever, fall for a guy like that. She would not show. She wouldn't. The smartest thing to do, the easiest, would be to get back on his Huffy and ride, ride away. But before the thought was fully formed…*there was Jenny.*

She approached along Division Street with the skinny blond, Sheila, Bobby didn't like. On the railing, Kevin and the others greeted the girls with hoots and hollers.

Leave her alone, Bobby thought, she's not coming to see you. She's just passing by, just…

But then the girls returned their greetings. "Hey, Kevin!" Bobby heard Jenny call. Why was she talking to him? And why was she walking that way, all twisty and girlish? Sheila, too, the two of them, both, giggling and flirting like the older girls Bobby had seen on other occasions at the bridge. Girls his mother would call *"loose."* This was not *his* Jenny.

Bobby watched with his heart in his throat—Jenny, the girl he loved, bouncing up onto the railing, her hair dancing in that wonderful way; Jenny dropping an arm around Kevin's shoulder; Jenny taking the bottle and swigging it back, giggling, ruffling Kevin's wavy hair.

Bobby wanted to run, get back on his bike and ride, ride away, escape the hurt, the pain…*the tormenting truth.* But he could not.

The night passed and the bridge party escalated, the girls bringing new life to the festivities. Like dogs in heat the boys were acting. Cecil howled at the stars. Buddy Seitz *honked* with laughter. Kevin preened machismo, taunting the girls.

"Come on!" Bobby heard Kevin urge. "You know you want to." He heard Jenny giggle in reply, a songbird's trill. "My Mom would kill me, Kevin." Sheila chimed in, saying, "Come on, Jenny, jeez, don't be so 'June Cleaver' about it. Let's go."

With Jenny's hesitant nod, the boys sprang down from their perch on the railing. Kevin took Jenny by the hand and led her. The others followed.

They crossed around the outside of the railing to where a path began and led downward. Bobby had seen the path before but never dared explore it. One-by-one they disappeared. Bobby could hear them laughing, cursing as they stumbled in the darkness somewhere beyond the railing.

Bobby sat in hiding. Loneliness, anger, shame devoured him, ate at him from the inside like a grotesque, hungry parasite. He knew the path would lead to the bottom of the ravine, to the base of the huge concrete columns, the supporting wooden trestles. He had heard stories that, if you were daring enough, you could climb the timbers, pick and choose them, as one might pick a path through the forest, to eventually reach the high ledge, atop the concrete pillars. There, hidden away beneath the surface of the roadway, the ledge became a secret fortress of sorts, available only to those courageous enough, strong enough, to make the climb. Dark and private.

"*Don't go near the bridge!*" Bobby heard his mother's voice echo in the night once more.

It had become cold in the alley or so it seemed. Bobby pulled his windbreaker tighter and drew himself from shadow to make his way across Division Street. At the railing, he paused to peer down the path. The voices of the others could be heard coming from somewhere down there in the darkness below.

By the time Bobby reached the bottom of the ravine the others had disappeared. Their muffled laughter had shifted upward, high atop one of the concrete columns. Thick, rough wooden beams pointed the way. Bobby tested the structure. Splinters bit into his palms.

"*Don't go near the bridge, Bobby.*"

He wanted to turn back, knew he should; yet his anger, boiling within him, prevented it.

Carefully Bobby mounted the trusses. Beam-by-beam, one treacherous move at a time, he picked his way upward. And upward still, the laughter from above growing more distinguishable with each rise.

At last, near the top, Bobby wedged himself into the crotch of two adjoining beams and peered into the darkness. He saw nothing, but he could hear their sounds easily, now, some fifteen feet away, atop the concrete column. He heard

Cecil howl with delight, heard Jenny giggle. Sheila's bleached-blonde voice cackled demonically. Their laughter was ugly to his ears, reminding Bobby of his uncle Bill's pig wallow. Bobby was young and inexperienced, but he imagined every kind of sinful revelry unfolding.

Bobby wished he could do something, maybe shake the bridge like a giant might do to get their attention, make it stop. And, as if wishing made it so, the bridge began to tremble, then shake. The shaking intensified, causing Bobby to clutch tighter to his supports. A deep resonance filled the ravine. The sound grew steadily louder, more powerful. And Bobby realized it was not wishful thinking that had set the bridge ashake, but the approach of a train. From beyond the curve, huge *chubbing* diesels were recognizable now. The laughter from the loft was all but lost in the closing swell.

The train rounded the bend and headed into the gap. Light burst forth, illuminating the bridge. Bobby closed his eyes against the brightness. He could hear the teens: *"All aboard! Whoo, whoo!"* Cecil was crying. Kevin called, "Chattanooga Choo-Choo!" then launched into his rendition of the song. The girls giggled, *Buddy honked.*

Bobby opened his eyes.

He could see the ledge now. And he could see his classmates. Shadows and light jittered and bounced and mixed with the vibration of the bridge and the train's forward motion. It gave the scene a surreal flickering quality, like that of an old time, silent movie. Bobby watched with anger as the teens frolicked in stuttering slow motion. There was Sheila rollicking shamelessly with Buddy Seitz and Cecil Johnson. Beyond, Jenny danced with Kevin. They jitterbugged, in strobe effect, as Kevin bleated out the rhythm. Jenny was holding Kevin close. They spun and dipped together in the spotlight as the train approached. Heavy sexual tension filled the air. It spread over Bobby and pressed at him. The relentless drive of the oncoming train added weight to it. A smothering heat followed. His head spun dizzily.

The ledge now sparked with carnal energy. The concrete columns danced and jived, thrust lewdly, to some erotic jungle beat. The timbers danced. Before Bobby's eyes, the bridge had become a living thing: a howling, surging entity.

Then suddenly, without warning, the bridge's mood changed.

Gnarly wooden fingers shot out to grab first at Sheila. She screamed then choked audibly as sharp wooden shards broke loose and sliced her throat. Liquid crimson splattered the beams and pooled on the concrete. Suckers quickly sprouted from the timbers and dined on her flesh, taking her into the rough old wood to become part of it.

The bridge turned on the others. Cecil's arms were severed from their sockets and tossed to the tracks before the fast approaching train. Buddy Seitz was gutted like the pig that he was. Then Kevin—his pretty head, decapitated. All were mutilated and devoured and sucked into the dancing timbers. And finally Jenny. Rope like wooden fingers spun out from the beams to encircle her throat and tighten.

The train plowed through the gap, picked up speed on its downhill run. The light that had spotlighted the horror passed quickly and departed, leaving the bridge once more in darkness. The rhythmic *clickity-clack* of the trailing cars continued, then they too faded down the tracks. The sudden heat wave vanished on their tail. The trembling ceased. And the night was still and cool once more…

Robert Anderson came out of his trance as the last veil of daylight settled beyond the horizon. Without realizing, he had somehow made his way down what was left of the treacherous old path and climbed the aging trusses to the ledge beneath the roadbed of the old bridge. He stood among the timbers, those upright supports that had haunted a lifetime of dreams. The bridge knew the secrets of that night and had harbored them alone these long years. And now the bridge had given them up to Robert.

He saw the way it had actually been that night, some thirty years ago. When his anger had boiled hot and bitter for the teenage boys, and for the skinny blond, whose devil-speak had encouraged their evil play. And for Jenny, the carnal temptress, who had betrayed his love.

That night, that fatal night, when Bobby had carried his father's hunting knife to the bridge—just in case—for protection. That night when his shame and humiliation would not be repressed.

Robert Anderson stared at the decaying wood. Funny, he thought. If you tilt your head, just so, if you catch the light, just right, you could still see them here. Those teens among the textures of the beams, like faces in knotty pine paneling. There was Kevin and Cecil. There was Buddy and Sheila.

And of course…there was Jenny.

The Bridge first appeared in 2004 Winter Issue of Futures Mysterious Anthology Magazine. It was Third Place Finalist in 2003 Fire To Fly Competition.

MOTHERHOUSE

Little Earl sat at the kitchen table, near the window, sorting through stacks of prints. There was a low, even din of white noise that was always there—traffic on the Hollywood Freeway and the general grind along Beverly. There were strong dinnertime cooking smells that changed with the shifting of the wind. Napping at his feet was *Blind Melon Dog*—a terrier-mongrel-mix, sightless and arthritic, with hair covering its eyes.

"What do you think, Melon?" Earl said, holding one of the eight-by-tens near floor level for the dog to consider. "Not bad for a poor dumb black man, huh? I say the pretty *Miss Melrose Lady* will like this one?"

The photo, taken through the windshield of a Lexus, showed a blonde woman from the suburbs making a drug purchase from a local street dealer. The dealer, a young black man, was leaned through the window; money and drugs were exchanging hands. Visible in the background was a child seat. The photo's passion came from the sadness evident in the moment.

Melon lifted his chin from his paws long enough to sniff the photo, whine once, and return to his nap.

Earl withdrew the photo to re-evaluate it. Nodding, he said, "Okay, I see what you're saying. But let's keep it for now, see what else we got."

The building where Earl lived had become his gallery. Framed photographs lined the hallways and stairwells and hung in neighboring units. In his own tiny apartment, more photographs stood lined along the baseboards and hung drying from wires inside the closet that had been converted into a darkroom. All were black-and-white glossies, all were graphic commentaries on life—life on the streets of Westlake, beyond the confines of *Motherhouse*.

From where Earl sat, four floors above Westmoreland Street, he could see out the window to the end of the block in both directions and out to where Council rounded north beyond the school. In the school parking lot, two cars sat in evening shade near the fence line. At the open trunk lid of one of the vehicles, a couple of Hispanic kids were hawking handguns to a tall, lanky black man. One of the kids did the talking, letting the black man sample the wares, while the other kid stood watch.

Earl observed them for a moment, then rose and crossed to the living area to where a black leather bag sat open near the sofa. Inside was a pair of cameras. He chose the Nikon with the telephoto lens and returned to the window. Sighting through the lens, Earl zeroed in on the black man, watched him heft an automatic in both hands and sight along the barrel. Earl clicked off a series of shots letting the auto-winder do the work, then turned the lens on the Hispanic kid beside the open trunk.

"What do you think, Melon, he a Rosebush? An AC/DC? Looks more like *Rolling Sixty-Four* to me, way outside his turf."

Earl set the camera aside. "I know what you're thinking," he said to Melon. "But that's street business. Ain't none of our'n." Earl returned to his work. *Blind Melon Dog* remained unmoved.

Three weeks earlier, Earl had been taking pictures of a homeless woman, nursing her child in an alley, when the pretty Miss Melrose Lady honked and waved him to her Mercedes. She'd been watching him from the street where the traffic was backed up at the light.

In the alley, the woman—a black woman—sat hunkered with her back against a dumpster. A drainpipe at the side of the building emptied run-off near her feet. The stream flowed beneath her sandals and soaked the hem of her dress where it hung to the pavement. The horn caused her to look up to see Earl with his camera trained on her. Without shame, she freed one breast from her bodice and shoved it into the crying infant's mouth. Earl snapped off a series of shots: moving, stooping, changing angles. Only when the film roll was done did he stop. And only then did he turn to the car at the curb.

She was in her late forties, hair blonde and layered, just off the neck. She wore designer jeans and an expensive silk blouse that flashed red lace above a swell of white flesh. Earl's first thought was that she was some rich housewife, bored with running the kids to recitals and swim class. But, no, she wanted to ask him about his work. Earl squatted beside the passenger door and looked across the seat at her.

"I saw you snapping photos. That's a very interesting subject you've chosen," the woman said.

Earl glanced to the woman in the alley, then back to the stylish lady in the car. He felt suddenly shabby, suddenly exposed, and in response fussed with the collar of his shirt.

"I take pictures what I see," Earl said.

"Character studies?"

"I guess. The neighborhood mostly. You know, people in it, the buildings that express its culture."

"You any good?" the woman asked.

Earl shrugged.

"I tell you what," the lady said, reaching her card to him. "Give me a call. I'd like to see some of your work."

Leaned across the seat that way, Earl could see down the front of her blouse. It was hard to look away, but he did, averting his eyes to the card and taking it from her.

"You want me to call you?"

"Mornings are best," the Melrose Lady said. And with that, pointed the Mercedes into traffic and was gone.

Earl remained squatting at the curb: *Jolana Kobel,* the card read, *Melrose Galleries.* It was two weeks before he got up the nerve to call.

Here it was going on eight p.m. Earl finished sorting the photos. He'd come up with twelve prints for the Melrose Lady—his better work as judged by him and his blind dog. Night had settled on Westmoreland Street. The dinnertime cooking smells had faded with the wind, as had the gun dealers in the schoolyard. With darkness, a kind of high-tension hum came into the neighborhood. Taggers could be seen dodging between the buildings with their spray paint, and low-chopped street riders with their elaborate murals and deep tinted windows made patrolling passes along the street.

Earl took up a fine-tip Sharpie and scrawled "Little Earl" in the corner of the chosen prints. He slipped them into clear protective sheet covers and hooked them neatly into a vinyl three-ring school binder, one he'd found at the Ninety-nine Cent Store for fifty cents.

"Go find your blanket," Earl said to Melon, slipping into his jacket. "Go on."

Melon whined a protest but struggled to his feet. He crossed the apartment, navigating blindly by gliding his shoulder along the sofa corners and table legs. Finding the bed, he took time to gauge the distance, then made a valiant leap into it, circling twice before settling with his chin once more on his paws. Earl shook his head. He gathered his cameras into the bag, tucked the school binder under his arm, and left the apartment.

From Westlake, it was a straight shot out Wilshire Boulevard into Beverly Hills, but it took the bus almost an hour to get there. Earl got off at La Cienega and walked the lighted boulevard to Starbucks where they'd agreed to meet. It was nine p.m. and the pretty Miss Melrose Lady hadn't arrived yet. Earl bought coffee and took a seat to wait.

Finally, at nine-thirty, the Mercedes blew into view on Wilshire, Jolana Kobel on her cell phone, making the corner on squealing tires and disappearing into the parking lot at the back.

Earl waited. Then waited some more.

Jolana Kobel finished her call on the walk in, looking for a tall black man that she could scarcely remember. But, now, recognized him easily, at a table near the window, a school binder in his lap, a camera bag on the floor beside him.

"Good to see you, Earl," she said, extending her hand to the man who rose politely to greet her.

He was dressed in a worn poplin work jacket, his name embroidered on the breast. His pants and shirt were also worn, but they were clean.

Jolana called her order across the room, then took the seat opposite him. "Jeez, I had to fight traffic all the way here. What about you?"

"I took the bus," Earl said.

"From Westlake?"

"From wherever I am," Earl said.

Jolana nodded.

"Do you work for a living?"

"I'm a janitor at the hospital," Earl said. "Clean floors."

"Well, there's nothing wrong with that," she said.

Jolana couldn't imagine this man with a toilet brush in his hands. He was aging, a little thin on top and graying at the temples. Still, he was big and powerful and looked as though he could work outdoors, road construction maybe.

She said, "Well…do you have something for me?"

"Before I show you my work," Earl said. "There's something I think it's only fair to tell you."

"Yes, what is it?"

"I did time, once."

"Prison?"

Earl nodded.

"Oh," Jolana said.

"You want to know what for, don't you?"

Jolana guessed he saw the question in her eyes, or maybe he'd just heard it all before. She said, "Okay, what for?"

Earl said, "Something, I shouldn't have been doin' when I was young. Breaking and entering."

Jolana said, "Okay," not knowing quite what else to say.

"That was a long time ago," Earl said. "I've known better for a long time now. You still want to see my work."

Jolana looked Earl in the eyes. There was a softness to them, hidden by a tired weariness. She said, "Earl, the only thing I'm qualified to judge is art. Would you like to show me yours?"

She watched him survey her carefully before turning the school binder to face her. Jolana opened it to the first photo.

"This is the one you were shooting on the street when I met you," she said.

"I thought you'd ask about it," Earl said.

Jolana studied the content, the woman nursing her baby, then held the binder away, imagining the photo framed and hanging from a gallery wall. *Mother and Child*—she imagined the caption beneath it reading.

"Earthy, very earthy. It's got something of a Bourke-White quality to it."

Earl said, "She taking care of her baby first. That's what I see."

"Uh-huh, uh-huh, I see what you're saying," Jolana said.

One of the Starbuck's staff delivered Jolana's latte, placing a napkin on the table with it. Jolana flipped the page, ignoring the drink and the server.

The next shot was the one taken through the windshield of the Lexus, the street dealer and the suburb lady making a drug buy. *The Market*—she envisioned the caption. The picture across the fold was that of a tagger, a member of the AC/DCs street gang, Earl mentioned to her, crafting gang signs along the arch of the highway overpass.

"My God, these look more like evidence than art," Jolana said. "But they're good, Earl…very good."

Jolana flipped the page to a close-up of a bearded wino. His toothless grin was shameless. His eyes twinkled mischievously.

She flipped again, her mind jumping to more captions and positions on the gallery wall.

There was a mother pushing a baby stroller past a neon-lighted liquor store. Nearby, a gathering of prostitutes watched her pass. One appeared to be whispering a confidence to another. *Envy*.

On another page was a shirtless white man with a needle in his vein. On another, a local street soldier was into his gangster slouch and almost invisible behind the wheel of his low rider. And there was a photo of an outdoor basketball hoop set against a bleak November sky, the net, ragged and torn and hanging by a single string.

Jolana flipped again.

"What's this one?"

Earl leaned over the photo. "That's the building where I live."

"It looks like a castle. Is it part of the Historical Register?"

Earl shrugged. "Historical to me. Been livin' there thirty-seven years. '*Motherhouse*' what I call her. The name on the sign out front say she the Normandy Apartment Building. See, that's my window, up there, looking down on the street."

"It's remarkable."

Jolana studied the photo a moment longer then closed the binder. "I have to say, Earl, they're very good. Are you currently showing?"

"Showing?" Earl said.

"Are your photos being displayed anywhere, in a gallery?"

"Just Motherhouse, my apartment. The neighbors have a few, you wanna call that *showing*."

Jolana leaned forward resting her elbows atop the portfolio. He had set her back with his confession, but she liked Earl, just the same, and she liked his work. "I'd like to show them, Earl. Melrose Gallery on Beverly Glen," she said.

"Sell my photos…?"

"I'd take the standard fee of course."

She watched him consider. "I don't know. See, I mostly take them for me. Ain't never thought of sellin'."

Jolana studied him. "You have no idea how much money you could make, do you?"

"Maybe I do," Earl said.

"Is that what scares you?"

"Who says I'm scared?"

"Well, it just seems odd to me you wouldn't want to make some money from your art.

Earl stood. He reached down and freed the binder from beneath Jolana's elbow. "I think my bus be coming soon. Need to get home in time to take Melon his walk."

"Melon?"

"Blind Melon Dog," Earl said. "Named him after the jazz artist Blind Melon Walker."

"That's cute, Earl. But look..." Jolana seemed to measure her words, "I really like your work, really. I believe it would sell. You have my card; just promise me you'll think about it."

Earl strung his camera bag over his shoulder, then nodded and walked off.

Jolana took up her latte, that had by now turned luke warm, and watched him go. She'd seen a lot of talent in her time. Prison or no prison, Little Earl had potential.

On the sidewalk, Earl stopped to breathe the air. Man, what was he thinking, turning the nice lady down? Maybe he was afraid, like she'd said.

Earl thought about it.

Naw, man, that ain't it. Look around, he told himself. This place nothin' like the neighborhood, nothin' like the people in your pictures. Wouldn't be fair, offer them up for social commentary like so many bug samples in a jar. Earl shook his head. On the other hand, he had to save every spare dime just to pay for film and developer. There was no denying he could use the money.

Earl stood thinking for a moment longer, the cars on Wilshire whipping by. Then tucking the school binder beneath his arm and hoisting his camera bag higher, he started the trek to the corner bus stop. He wasn't quite sure what he should do, whether showing his photos would be some kind of betrayal or not. But he did know one thing. If he did talk to the pretty Miss Melrose Lady again...he'd ask her what "standard fee" meant.

Midnight, Naco found Little Dog outside Tony-Taco and told him he'd gotten word that Rollin' Sixty-Fours had been spotted earlier by the school. He had Leya, one of the home girls, in the car with him.

"There's two of them, Home," he said. "Let's roll."

They picked up Baby Mouth walking south down Virgil toward his house and now there were three of them and the girl. They made a sweep of the block down

Westmoreland and up Council past the school, then back around and up Westmoreland again. They cut across First Street to Vermont, then out Beverly past Fastfood Row looking for a dark green Monte Carlo.

"You sure they're around here, bitch," Naco said to Leya.

"Man, I told you. Ria said she saw two of them. Matro and that punk they call Racer. Sixty-Fours...and don't call me bitch, man! I'm not your bitch!"

"Yeah, well you're somebody's bitch."

"I belong to Ramone. And don't forget it, Naco."

Naco threw a glance across the seat at his Homies. "Ramone! Shit, huh," he said.

Little Dog and Baby Mouth made little response; they kept their eyes on the street. The four of them continued to roll.

It was a little after midnight when they spotted the green lowrider on Beverly and followed it back down Westmoreland past the apartment building that looked like a castle and the schoolyard where Leya said they had been seen earlier in the evening.

When the lowrider turned into the school parking lot, Naco continued on. Leya, keeping her eyes on the lowrider as they passed, said, "Shit, that's them, man. That's the fucking Fours were here earlier."

"Dudes got a couple of chicas in back," Little Dog said, looking back across his shoulder.

Naco let the car idle at the stop sign, watching the lowrider in his rearview mirror. It was doubling back, now, across the school parking lot toward the fence line across from the castle.

Naco watched for a moment longer, then made a right at the corner and circled the block. He killed the headlights as they came down Council, letting the car creep on its own. Up ahead, facing them was the castle: its stucco façade, its tall cylindrical tower with the cone-shaped roof that looked like a rocket ship about to be launched.

In the school parking lot, the two Sixty-Fours were outside of the car now. The two girls were sitting on the hood. They all had cans of beer in their hands, the remainder of a twelve pack sat on the roof.

Naco slid the car to the curb and quietly killed the engine.

"Check it out es'se," Little Dog said from the backseat. "Look like home girls Top Girl and Switch."

"That ain't right," Baby Mouth said. "They home girls, they should be riding with us, man."

"They're putas," Leya said, "You should be glad they with the Fours. Maybe give you the AIDS or something worse, man."

"What's worse than AIDS?" Baby Mouth asked.

"You go with them and see, chucho."

"What should we do?" Little Dog asked. His question was directed at Naco.

Naco watched the girls drinking and laughing with the vatos from outside the neighborhood. He let his eyes scan the street. There were a few lights on in some of the houses and apartments, but shades were drawn, there was no one on the street.

"Break it open," Naco said.

At his command, there was a flurry of activity inside the car: the sound of slides wracking, the smell of gun oil suddenly in the air.

"You stay here, chica," Naco said, pulling an automatic from beneath his seat. To the others he said. "Let's do it fast."

The young men slipped from the car and moved stealthily between the cars that were parked along the street. When they were in striking range, Naco gave them a sign, and the three charged onto the sidewalk.

The schoolyard came alive with the *pop-pop-pop* of automatic weapons. Muzzle flash lit the night. The smell of gun smoke bit the air.

The Hispanic boys, caught off guard, went down. The girls screamed and rolled from the hood of the car. The one called Top Girl scrambled on hands and knees across the pavement, then got her footing and ran; the other, Switch, collapsed into a fetal position on the pavement. She lay screaming as Naco and his boys emptied their weapons into the bodies of the boys that, now, lay motionless on the pavement.

When the gunfire ceased, silence settled over the neighborhood once more. A cloud of acrid smoke hung above the yard. Naco turned his gaze to the girl on the ground. "Don't let me see you anytime soon, chica! Comprende? Tell Top Girl too."

The girl—a mask of terror welded to her face—nodded.

Naco took a quick glance along the street; shades remained pulled, windows remained dark. "Let's go!" he said.

They were turning toward the car when something caught Naco's eye, movement from a window above the street. Naco turned to see the figure of a man, a tall black man, looking down at them from the top window of the castle. Alongside was a dog with his paws on the sill, his nose to the air. The dog let out a long shrill howl.

"Who's that?" Little Dog said.

Naco shook his head.

"You think he saw us?"

The three stood looking up at the figure, which seemed to raise something to his face. Off and away, police sirens rose.

Naco raised his gun to the window and sighted along the barrel. The figure didn't move. "Click," he said, and grinned. "He's too far away to identify shit. Let's go."

At the car, Little Dog and Baby Mouth piled quickly into the back seat. Naco paused to take a last glance toward the window. The man and the dog were gone. He was sure they were too far away to make identification. Still it nagged at him just the same.

Naco slid into the driver's seat. He took Leya's face in his hands and kissed her roughly on the mouth, letting his hand slide high up her thigh to work its way in deep between her legs.

Pulling away, Naco said, "You tell that faggot, Ramone, you belong to me now, chica."

Leya slid close to Naco and put her arm around him. Her hand slipped inside his shirt, her lips moved against his ear. Naco fired the engine, made a U in the street, and gunned them out of there.

The neighborhood lay quiet for the time. In the schoolyard, the two young Hispanic kids lay draining blood into the pavement. Through an alley somewhere a block over, Top Girl and Switch raced for their respective homes. And, as police sirens drew near, the light in the top floor castle window went dark.

Fashioned after a fourteenth century Norman castle, the Normandy Apartment Building had stood sentry over the One-Hundred block of Westmoreland Street for more than eight decades. It had seen the neighborhood change—first seeing it grow around her, then watching as it slowly slipped into decay. She, on the other hand, the "Motherhouse of Westlake," had remained strong and defiant, and was a source of pride to Earl and the other residents.

Oddly, this building that resembled a castle was also respected by the gangs who fought for control of the neighborhood. Up and down Westmoreland, all along Council, the walls and fences, light posts and sidewalks were tagged with gang markings. The school across the way also tagged. Only Motherhouse, the Grand Old Lady of the neighborhood, remained untouched by gang graffiti. Earl wasn't sure why. Perhaps the gangs had decided there was something sacred about her. Or perhaps something magical. All he knew was that he loved the Motherhouse and was proud to call her home.

On the evening following the shooting in the schoolyard, Little Earl arrived home from his shift, mopping floors at the hospital, to find gang signs scrawled across the stucco façade of Motherhouse. They were Rosebush markings, Earl recognized, the same gang who had run up on the Sixty-Fours partying in the schoolyard.

The next day, Earl brought home graffiti remover, stuff he found in a maintenance cabinet at the hospital, and scrubbed away the markings. That night the graffiti returned.

Earl felt his teeth clinch. Why this?

It had to do with him, he was certain of that—him witnessing the killings, that kid Naco pouring bullets into the two Hispanic kids from outside the neighborhood.

Yeah, Earl knew his name.

And this kid was trying to tell him something. "Man, you keep your mouth shut if you know what's good for you."

Earl did know what was good for him. Taking pictures was good for him. Motherhouse was good for him. And protecting her was good for him. What he had to do next, Earl thought, was teach this kid, Naco, what was good for *him.*

The next night, Earl's night off, he went into his closet-darkroom and developed his most recent roll of film. Blind Melon Dog lay in wait outside the door. When the prints were dry, he selected one eight-by-ten he liked best and came out.

"Melon," Earl said, "What say we take a little walk uptown?"

Melon struggled to his feet.

Earl took the print and scrawled his signature in the corner. He slipped it into a manila envelope, then, snapping a leash on Melon, took the envelope and the dog and went out into the night.

They headed up Beverly, the blind dog and his seeing-eye master, taking their time to get to Tony-Taco. It was the place Earl knew he would most likely find the Rosebushes.

The place was relatively dead when they arrived. One Hispanic man with his two small children ate out of wrappers at one of the outdoor tables. No sign of the Rosebushes. Earl bought a fountain drink and took a seat at one of the other tables. Melon found a spot on the pavement at his feet.

It was less the ten minutes before they appeared—the kid Naco in his chopped car, and the girl and two boys from the other night. A third boy, a fat Hispanic kid, was jammed in with them. They backed the car into a slot and piled into the lot in floppy shirts and baggie pants, ball caps turned backwards. Naco was in tight jeans and a black t-shirt, the girl in a denim jacket over wide Spandex.

"Get us some food, chica," Naco told the girl, as they crossed the lot.

"What I look like, chucho? I'm not your fucking *mucama*, man!" the girl said.

Earl watched as Naco grabbed the girl roughly by the arm and jerked her close. He said something through gritted teeth, then shoved her off toward the order window.

The girl stumbled, kept her feet, then fell into a defiant, feminine hip-swing, lifting one finger over her shoulder, as she moved off across the lot. Naco and the others took over the tables near the man with the children, taking seats on the table, crowding in and causing a stir. The man hustled his children through their meal and left with them.

Earl watched the boys as he sucked down the last of his drink. He gathered Melon by the leash and crossed toward them.

They saw him coming, their revelry diminishing, their eyes narrowing, as he approached.

"How you boys doing tonight?" Earl asked.

"Hey, where'd you get the dead dog, amigo?" one of the boys said

"He's old," Earl said, "just like me. And he's blind, the way you'd like me to be."

It was Naco who addressed him now. "Who the fuck are you, old man? What do you want here?"

"I'm a guy who sees things," Earl said.

"So you're telling me you're not blind like the dog? So what?"

"I'm telling you I see more than you want me too. And I know who you are too."

Naco studied Earl closely. "You the man in the window, am I right?" Naco said.

Earl nodded.

"You think you're a witness to something. That what you're saying? Maybe you wouldn't be such a good witness, you see more like your dog," Naco said.

Earl heard the unmistakable sound of a knife clicking open. And now the fat kid was stepping down off the table to circle behind him; he held a long slender blade near his leg.

"Before you do anything stupid, son," Earl said. "Maybe you should take a look at this first." Earl extended the envelope to Naco.

"What's this?"

"It's a present, for you," Earl said, gesturing for him to take it. "I thought you'd like to be the first on your block to own a *Little Earl.*"

Naco nodded to one his boys, who took the envelope from Earl to hand it to him. He slipped the photo out, stared at it.

The photo was a close-up of him, his face framed at the end of a telephoto lens, and looking up from the car. It was signed in the corner. Naco recognized the scene.

"What if we just took this and left you bleeding on the sidewalk?" Naco said. "What then?"

The others had come off the tables now also.

"There are more where these came from," Earl said, "and others that show the rest of what happened the other night."

"So what is it you want, man? You want to take me to jail, make a citizen's arrest?"

"No," Earl said. "I'm not looking to bring you down. There was a time when I wasn't so different from you. As far as I'm concerned, you and your soldiers here are as much a part of the culture of this neighborhood as anything else. It's life on the streets. I understand that. All I want is for you to keep your taggers off Motherhouse."

"The castle?"

"That's right, the castle. Stop the tagging and no one has to see the photos."

"Why's she so special?"

"You tell me," Earl said. "Until the other night, even you thought so."

"I tell you what, abuelo. You bring me the other photos and all the negatives, and I won't have to come looking for you."

"Is that your bargain?" Earl said.

"I don't bargain, old man. I'm just being nice to my elders and giving you some time to come clean with the goods, Home."

"No more graffiti."

"You love that Motherhouse, don't you? I'll tell you what, I'll think about it."

Earl turned, giving a tug on Melon's leash to get him going, and pushed off past the fat kid with the knife. He gave the kid a firm brush of his shoulder as he passed, just to let him know he wasn't intimidated. Earl headed down Beverly, with Blind Melon Dog in tow, feeling the eyes of the Rosebush Gang upon him.

Three days went by without fresh graffiti appearing on the face of Motherhouse. On several occasions, he had seen the chopped lowrider, the one Naco drove, pass by on the street below, but all things considered, it had remained quiet on Westmoreland Street.

By the fourth day, Earl had quit thinking about the Rosebushes and had started thinking once again about the pretty Miss Melrose Lady. On the fifth day, as if hearing his thoughts across town, she called, surprising him at the hospital where he worked.

"I don't know, ma'am," Earl said. "I'm still thinking about it."

"What's the problem, Earl, are you afraid people won't like your work?"

He couldn't explain it. He couldn't tell her how he felt it was like giving rich folks one more vantage from which to feel superior. He said, "I'm just not sure."

"Listen, Earl, I got an event scheduled for tomorrow evening but I don't think one of my artists is going to come through for me. Give me twenty or so of your best-framed photos and let's see how they do."

Earl hung up without saying yes or no, but promised, once again, to think about it. That night, arriving home from work, Earl was stopped in his tracks in front of the building.

The graffiti had returned to Motherhouse.

Naco saw the tall graying black man coming across the parking lot of Tony-Taco's toward them. He was there with only two of his boys, Little Dog and Baby Mouth. He roused them, saying, "Man, check it out."

He struck a casual pose, leaned back on his elbows, and waited. "What's happening, Home?" he said, as the big man who called himself Little Earl approached.

"I thought I told you no more tagging of Motherhouse."

"You told *me*...? No! I told you bring me the prints and negatives, and I won't have to turn my wolf pack loose on you, man." Naco turned a look to his boys, the two snickering beneath their breath.

Before he realized what was happening, Naco felt himself jerked off the table. "Hey, shit!" He heard himself say. And felt the man grab a handful of crotch and shirtfront all at once and lift him high overhead.

As Little Dog and Baby Mouth came off the table, Naco found himself flying through the air to crash broadside into the two of them. All three went down hard, Naco skinning his face and elbows on the pavement.

The three lay looking up at the black man, who was standing over them now, fists clenched.

"No more graffiti!"

The man turned without looking back and stalked away down Beverly.

Naco sprang to his feet. He circled in place, wiping blood from the scrape on his cheek. He turned to the departing figure, shaking a fist at the man's back. He called, "This ain't the end of it, old man! Pictures or no pictures, you better watch your back, Home!"

The following day Earl called Jolana Kobel and told her he'd have twenty framed photos ready by four p.m., delivered to her studio. Why the change of heart? Earl told her he'd seen the light was all.

Earl went about the apartment gathering framed photos into a canvass bag, then crossed to the kitchen table to collect his most recent work. They were the scenes of the schoolyard, two of them: guns blazing in the night, and Naco, close-up, his face filling the frame. Earl remembered Jolana saying his work looked more like evidence than art. It made him pause.

But why?

The shot of the shooting in the schoolyard was too broad, too pulled back, to provide any sort of specific identification. The close-up on the other hand said nothing, it was a face, nothing more, eyes narrowed and questioning.

Earl added the shots to the canvass bag. "Let the lady decide," he told Melon.

At four-thirty Earl stepped off the bus in Beverly Hills. In his best wool jacket, the canvass bag strung over his shoulder, Earl entered Melrose Gallery, getting looks from people on the street. He was greeted inside by an artsy looking young girl with short hair. "Hi, I'm Chris. You must be Earl," she said. "Jolana's expecting you."

They crossed into a spacious gallery. Hardwood flooring gleamed up at Earl. Track lights in the ceiling focused on framed artwork that lined the walls. Earl felt a new wave of apprehension wash over him.

"Maybe, I should just go..." he said, turning.

"Earl, "I'm so glad you could make it."

It was Jolana's enthusiastic voice calling to him. She'd come in through a wide doorway that led off into another section of gallery. She'd been working, obviously. She wore a loose fitting sweatshirt over black leotards, and was pushing fallen strands of hair from her eyes as she approached, hand extended.

Earl shook her hand, then unstrung the canvass bag from his shoulder and handed it to her.

"They the best I have, I guess," Earl said, "though now I'm not sure."

"Don't be shy, Earl, look around," Jolana said, taking the bag. "You belong here."

Earl let his eyes slide down the length of the studio. There were works of other artists on the walls. Some were photographs like his. Others were paintings. Still others were pen and ink drawings, pastel chalks, some watercolors. Earl saw something in each and every one of them. They were timid or bold, raw or refreshing. It didn't seem to matter. What mattered, he decided, was that each had something unique to offer, some perspective...like his. It eased his mind just a little.

"We'll let Chris get started hanging these," Jolana said, handing the bag over to the young girl, who took it and went off the through the doorway where Jolana had entered. "I've cleared some space in the South Gallery, and...Oh! Oh my gosh! I have to start getting ready too. Are you going to be staying to greet your public?"

Earl hadn't thought of staying, thought nothing of having a *public*. He said, "Naw, I need to get back. You know."

"Well, keep you fingers crossed," Jolana said. And dashed off to wherever it was women like her dashed off to.

Earl gave one last look at the various pieces of art that hung on the walls, then made his way out to find his bus ride home.

There was an immediate ring of tension in the air when Earl stepped off the bus in Westlake. Down Westmoreland Street there were flashing lights and people in the street, a huge crowd being contained near the schoolyard.

Earl began the walk downhill, keeping his eyes on the gathering, then broke into a jog as he noticed the cloud of smoke that was billowing skyward. He was running by the time he hit the bottom of the hill. Fire engines were positioned along the curb and hoses were strung from hydrants, Motherhouse—Christ!—alive with fire.

Earl stopped short.

"Where's Melon!" Earl cried. "Where's my dog!"

In the window that was once his apartment, Earl could see black clouds of gas and smoke belching forth; somewhere inside heard timbers crunching, walls collapsing.

Earl pushed through the crowd.

"You seen my dog? Have you seen Melon? Anybody seen a black and white mutt?"

He got blank looks from some, a shake of the head from others whose eyes were glued to the inferno. Earl made his way to the front of the crowd.

"That's far enough," a uniformed officer said.

"My dog," Earl said. "He was inside."

"I'm sorry, pal, but if he's in there now, he won't be coming out. We checked all the apartments, kicked in every door. Didn't see no dog and were just damn lucky to get all the tenants out."

"But he's blind," Earl said.

The uniformed officer gave Earl a shrug.

Earl watched the smoke pour from his apartment; watched sections of the castle façade give way. Minutes from now there would be nothing left: nothing of his home, his equipment, his photos, his life. All gone with Motherhouse and Melon.

Earl lowered his head.

Flames continued to roar, lights continued to twirl. He was about to turn away, when sudden murmuring from the crowd caused him to look up. It was like a ripple among them, an impromptu stadium-wave, moving his way. When the sea of onlookers parted, Earl saw Melon moving through the crowd, leading with his shoulder that grazed the shins and calves of the onlookers. His nose was in the air, sniffing, sorting the various smells, as he locked-onto and came to the one scent important to him.

Earl stooped and let Melon find him. The dog doing so quickly, burying his face in Earl's chest. Earl stroked his blind dog, whispering in his ear, reassuring him. And they remained that way until the last of Motherhouse was consumed.

Jolana Kobel was interrupted as she greeted guests to the showing, Chris leaning in close to say, "I'm sorry, but he says it's important."

She took the phone in the office.

"Earl?"

"I need you to come get my dog," Earl said on the other end of the line.

"What?"

"He's a good dog. Won't be no trouble to anybody."

Jolana shook her head to gather sense of it. "I don't understand, Earl. Why do I need to keep your dog?"

"'Cause I'm gonna be going away for a while. I didn't know who else to call."

"Well...okay, sure...I'll keep him for a while...I guess...but, why are you...?"

"Can you come get him now?"

"Now?" Jolana glanced out into the gallery where guests were starting to browse. "Earl, I'm right in the middle of the showing, this is your big chance."

There was silence on the line. Jolana relented. "All right, Earl. If it's that important to you, I guess Chris can handle things here. Where shall I meet you?"

"I won't be there, but there's a Tony-Taco, close to where you first saw me taking photos. Just look for a black and white mutt don't see so good. Say 'Melon.' He hears his name, he'll come to you."

"Melon...all right, Earl...but I don't understand. Where will you be?"

The line went dead. Jolana held the phone away and stared into it with dismay.

What the hay...? This man she'd met barely a week or so ago was suddenly, unexpectedly, asking her to come get his dog—Christ!—leave her guests in the middle of a showing—his showing!—and come get his dog. Worse, she'd said yes.

Jolana set the phone receiver back in its cradle.

Earl. He seemed like a nice man. A helluva talent. But what did she know about him? What really? He'd said he'd served time, and now talked in cloaked terms about *going away* for a while.

Jolana looked out into the gallery where a group of guests were now gathered before Earl's photos, displayed and accented by track lighting, on the wall. She let her gaze come back. Then, and only then, did she notice the one framed photo lying on her desk, a Post-It note attached in Chris's hand writing. *Do you really want to display this one?* the note read.

Jolana peeled away the note and stared at a wide-angle shot that appeared to have been taken looking down. Her mind leaped to a view of it hanging on the gallery wall. *Gunfire In The Night* she saw captioned beneath it. Suddenly, she knew what she had to do.

It took Earl fifteen minutes to reach Tony-Taco with Melon gathered in his arms. Naco and two of his boys were there and waiting for him, as he'd expected, leaned against Naco's lowrider. But now they came to their feet and stepped forward.

"We have been es'pecting you, old man," Naco said.

Earl crossed to the outdoor tables and deposited Melon on one of the concrete benches. "Stay," he said in a low voice, and Melon settled on his haunches.

Now Earl turned his attention to the Hispanic teens. He traversed the parking lot to come within three feet of Naco and the other two.

"You shouldn't have done what you did," Earl said.

"Which *did* is that, man? Kill those two vatos invading our turf, or burn down your house."

"I stay out of your business," Earl said. "You should have left it that way."

"Man has a thing for crazy old buildings," the teen on the right said.

"So, what now, old man?" Naco said.

"I'm going to give the two of them the chance to walk away. Then you and I are going to take a walk down that alley back there and settle this."

Naco lifted his shirttail, discreetly revealing the butt of a handgun. He gave Earl time to see it, before dropping his shirt back over it.

"You sure you don't want to walk away, amigo," Naco said.

Earl took a step forward. In the instant before he reached Naco, he heard the click of a blade and saw the teen on the right lunge toward him. He felt the cold of steel as the blade sunk deep into his side, felt the white hot flash of pain that followed. Earl grabbed hold of the teen's knife hand before he could pull back, clamped down on it with vise like strength, until the teen let go and stumbled back against the car.

Earl withdrew the blade from his side, feeling the rush of blood that followed. Now he held it to Naco. "My blood for yours," Earl said.

There was a moment of uncertainty in Naco's eyes before he grabbed for his gun. Earl reached him before he could clear the weapon from beneath his shirt. He threw one big arm around the kid's neck and spun him to face away, then brought the knife blade to his throat. Earl dragged the teen several steps back with him across the parking lot, increased the pressure on his hold.

"Drop the gun," Earl said into Naco's ear.

Naco did, the gun banging, then clattering on the concrete.

"Now, tell your buddies to take a hike."

Naco said nothing and Earl drew the blade up tighter against Naco's throat, taking skin with it and causing blood to trickle down his neck.

"Go! Vamos! Get out of here!" Naco shouted at them.

The two teens hesitated but then turned and ran off toward the alley behind Tony-Taco.

Earl drew the knife even tighter. He could feel blood throbbing in his temples, could feel more blood running from his wound down the front of his leg. He could see Melon slumped on his paws, a wide-eyed Hispanic girl behind the order-window, frantic what to do. He'd done time once for his stupidity and it had taken the better part of his life away.

"That apartment house was my Mother, man!" Earl said to Naco. "You understand? Everything I own was in her."

"So, what now, es'se? You gonna kill me?" Naco said. The words choked off as Earl squeezed harder.

"I'd like to," he said. "Slit your throat right here. And if my dog had burned in that fire, you'd have already been dead."

Earl watched Naco's eyes shift to Melon lying on the concrete table. Saw something in them that brought back memories from long ago. A young street kid—himself—scared and desperate.

"I could send you to prison with what I know, but I don't wish that on anybody. No," Earl said, "enough."

Earl withdrew the blade from the kid's throat and shoved him away. "It's over. Go on get out of here."

Naco stood glaring, rubbing the wound at his throat, then turned toward his car.

"Not that way!" Earl said. "The way your buddies did, on foot!"

Naco turned to look at him, then turned toward the alley. Over his shoulder, he said, "Ain't nothing over, man. Next time, maybe, the dog dies!"

Earl stooped to retrieve the gun from the pavement and leveled it at the back of Naco's head.

"Earl, no!" a voice said.

It stopped him. Stopped the kid, Naco, too.

Earl glanced over his shoulder to see Jolana Kobel standing outside the open door of a police car. The driver of the car, a young Asian cop, was out now too, his gun leveled across the roof of the car. Other police cars were joining them.

"This one ain't ever gonna stop," Earl said.

"Whatever this is about, Earl, it's not worth it, don't do it!"

"Put the gun down, Mister," the Asian cop said.

"Do what you want to me," Earl said. "Just make sure you take care of Melon." Earl turned his attention back to Naco.

"Earl don't!"

Earl cocked the gun.

He was about to pull the trigger, when he felt something familiar at his leg. Earl looked down to see Blind Melon Dog, who, having heard his name, had come and was now working figure eights at Earl's feet: swiping first one of Earl's shins with his shoulder, then the other...

He swiped first one of the guest's shins, then the other, a young preppy looking couple who looked as though they had just stepped off a wedding cake: the woman in tennis whites, the man in expensive slacks with a sweater draped, rather than worn, over his Calvin Kline shirt.

Jolana said, "This is the artist, Little Earl, I've been telling you about. I'll leave you to chat, but if you and your wife are any sort of collectors at all, James," Jolana whispered in confidence, "you'll want several of his works."

"Awww, look at the puppy," the young woman said, stooping to stroke Melon beneath the chin.

"They have a kind of Bourke-White quality to them," the husband said, studying one of Earl's photos on the wall, "the power that only comes from black and white. Urban, very urban."

Earl, in a black tuxedo, his hands clasped politely in front of him, said, "These are all 'one offs.' The negatives were destroyed in a fire."

"Really, how interesting," the man said, moving along the row of prints, his wife standing now to join him, arm in arm.

They stopped in front of one print in particular. "I like this one. 'Motherhouse' the caption reads. How intriguing. How much are you asking?"

"That's my favorite too," Earl said. "Modeled after a great Norman Castle. But it's not for sale."

"Not for sale? But we must have it, don't you think, Renee?"

The young woman shrugged, held her hand down for Melon to lick.

"Name your price," the man said to Earl.

Earl gave it some thought, pretending to study the print himself. "All right, if you insist—I'll let it go for five."

"Five thousand?"

"All right," Earl said.

"Look, Sweety, we own a 'Little Earl.'"

Earl smiled. "Just see Chris, the young lady at the desk. She'll write it up."

They shook hands, Earl and the preppy young man, Earl and the clueless wife, and Earl watched the couple stroll away. *His public*, he thought.

Earl took one last look at the photo. *Motherhouse*. It would be tough giving her up. She had been his home for more than thirty-seven years. But what the hell, Earl thought. Maybe now she'd have a fine home of her own.

The End

978-0-595-37783-1
0-595-37783-1

Printed in the United States
46830LVS00007B/253-306

Nuccio struck a pose, appearing to give it some thought. He shook his head. "No...I don't think so. I would have remembered that. What else you got?"

It wasn't turning out at all like Fremont had imagined—cool and controlled. This guy, this big-knuckled Guinea with the attention span of a four-year-old, all those videos—they were throwing him off his game. Lougie sitting there, hat-in-hand, the way he was, not adding anything.

Fremont came to his feet. "Looky here, man!" he said, placing his hands flat on Nuccio's desk, leaning in. "You need to shape your punk-ass and listen!"

"I don't know what that means," Nuccio said. "You want to try speaking English."

"Means you're in deep shit you don't pay attention!" Fremont was frothing now.

"Alright, alright. Sit down."

Nuccio waved Fremont back into his seat. He studied Fremont for a second then dropped his feet off the desk and came around to lean on his elbows, his attention focused on him politely. "So you popped the crusading Councilman. Tell me...what's that got to do with me?"

Fremont settled. He collected his cool, once more adjusted his cuffs. "You were seen making threats against the Councilman on national television, and now he's dead. All it takes is one anonymous phone call from us to say where the body is and you'll be on the hot seat for it."

"They'd have to make a case, prove I did it."

"Oh, they'll have proof alright. See it was your gun did the deed."

"My gun?"

Lougie looked up for the first time. He said, "From your nightstand."

Nuccio threw him a glance and Lougie went back to studying the lines in his palm.

"That's right!" Fremont continued. "And that very gun will be found with the body, your fingerprints all over it."

Thus far, Nuccio had been observing them with an air of calm amusement, now his face changed, his eyes narrowed, a vein at his temple began to pulse. "What is it you want?"

"We got you by the balls," Fremont said, "and we want some cash. Fifty...no...make that seventy-five thousand."

Nuccio pushed back in his chair and stood. His eyes ran from Fremont to Lougie. "Let me get this straight," Nuccio said. He turned to pace several steps away, seeming to think about it before turning again. "You broke into my private quarters to steal my gun, so you could use it to kill Hornackey, make it look like it was me who did it. Now you want money to keep it quiet. Am I understanding this right?"

Fremont returned Nuccio's gaze without comment.

"What happens I pay you the money and the body shows up anyway? I'm still in deep shit."

"Cause once you give us the cash, we tell you where the body is, you can dispose of it your own way, recover the gun, toss it in the river, whatever. Don't guys like you have one of those *Cleaning Crews*?"

"Cleaning crew," Nuccio said, making sure he heard it correctly.

"Yeah, like in the movies, man," Fremont said. "Team comes in, disposes of the body, cleans up the blood, the prints, tosses the evidence."

"Oh, yeah, Cleaning Crew," Nuccio said.

"Either way, you'll know where the gun and the body is and can do your own thing with it, eliminate the evidence."

"And what if I decide, instead, to just cap the two of you right here? No phone calls to the authorities, life goes on."

Fremont turned to Lougie giving him a nudge on the shoulder. "Man says he's thinking of popping the two of us instead." Lougie gave-up an oafish laugh, but he sat up straight to pay attention now.

Turning back to Nuccio, Fremont said, "You could do that, sure, have the two of us popped. But run the risk of the body being found on its own, accidentally."

Nuccio rubbed his chin, giving the situation some thought. Then to Fremont, said, "One time, seventy-five thou? You tell me where the body's hidden and I don't see you guys ever again?"

"Like ghosts in the night, we'll be gone. Look at it as a business transaction. You didn't like the do-good Councilman, he was getting in the way of your land development projects, so we simply took care of a sticky problem for you. Consider it payment for services rendered."

There was a long dry moment between them, Nuccio holding Fremont's gaze. Fremont wasn't sure how much longer he could keep it together. Coming back at the man, eye to eye, but inside beginning to unravel. Finally, Nuccio nodded. "Services rendered, sure, why not."

Fremont let himself breath a little as Nuccio returned to his seat and fished a bulky paper sack from the desk drawer. From it, he dumped banded bundles of money onto the desk—lots of it. Fremont exchanged a glance with Lougie, the two of them wide-eyed, awed by the availability of so much cash.